A LOVE DIVIDED

MARY'S LADIES, BOOK 1

BELLE MCINNES

Eden
Press

Printed in the United Kingdom
First published, 2017
This edition, 2020
Cover by Alba Covers

Find out more about Belle and her upcoming books by joining her
newsletter:
subscribepage.com/joinbelle

For Catherine, an inspirational dressage trainer, taken too soon.

CONTENTS

ABOUT THIS BOOK

Mary Queen of Scots is on the throne, and the frontier between England and Scotland is a powder-keg

More interested in raiding into Scotland with the rest of her clan than womanly pursuits like embroidery or finding a husband, Alexandra Graham is a feisty English heiress who rides and fights as well as any man. But when a daring rescue goes wrong, she ends up in the dungeons of Scotland's most forbidding castle, prisoner of the notorious Earl of Bothwell and at the mercy of the queen's justice.

As deputy warden responsible for keeping the law on the queen's borderland, Michael Cranstoun is a Scottish laird with a reputation for fair-mindedness and the looks of a Viking warrior. But when he meets the beguiling Alexandra, both his life and his honour are at risk—not to mention his affections.

With more than just the border separating them, Alex and Michael are on opposite sides of an ancient divide, and destined for different paths. But a shared love for horses draws them together and kindles a passion that respects no boundaries, and endangers more than just their hearts...

MAP

SCOTLAND IN THE TIME OF MARY
QUEEN OF SCOTS

CHAPTER 1

THURSDAY 3RD OCTOBER, 1566

ALEX BENT LOW over the black stallion's neck, trusting his sure-footedness as they sped over the moonlit moor, driving the small herd of rangy cattle before them.

From her left came a muffled curse, as Hob Forster's horse tripped on a mole hill. Only luck and a handful of mane kept him safely on his mount's broad back, his teeth glinting white in the shadows of his round face as he grinned with delight at the near miss. Like Alex, he was dressed in leather boots, breeches and an iron breastplate, with a steel helmet pulled down over his ears, sword at his side and longbow over his shoulder.

If they hadn't been sworn to silence by the fierce black eyebrows of their leader, Iron Simon Graham, Alex could've laughed at the danger and excitement of it all. For how many Border lasses were allowed to join their kinsmen on a raid into enemy country? And how many women could sit a horse as well as she, or fire an arrow as fast and true? And how many women could claim the leader as their father, or

1

twist him around their little finger till he capitulated to their request to join the band? *Not many!*

But surely they should be past the worst of the danger, now that they'd left the sheltered Liddesdale glen with its stone-walled cattle pen and sleeping Elliot guards? Wouldn't they now be safe to shout or cheer or sing of their victory?

She glanced over her shoulder. *No,* perhaps not.

Here on foreign soil, a reiver could never be too careful—especially when they'd 'liberated' over a dozen cattle from an opponent's stockade and were still half a mile from the border—and further still from home turf, a safe house and a warm bed.

A distant yell and the muffled rumble of galloping hooves sent Alex's pulse racing and proved that her caution was well founded. Far down the valley, in the wake of the band of Grahams and Forsters and their ill-gotten cattle, a bunch of dark shapes—which could only be their Elliot foes—raced to catch up with the English reivers.

Hooves sank into softer ground as Alex's kinsmen hurried the cattle towards the ford over Liddel Water—the river that, in this area, acted as a physical expression of a boundary that existed on maps and in the hearts and minds of royalty. But for the Border tribes, the border was a notional thing; to be deployed when convenient and ignored where appropriate.

Like now.

Alex didn't delude herself that the border would be any more a barrier to their Scots pursuers than it was to Iron Simon's band of English reivers. They needed speed, deception—and some luck.

Clattering and splashing through the shallow river, they urged their mounts and the tiring cattle along the narrow valley of Kershope.

Iron Simon and Evan, his brother, rode at the front, leading the band at this critical point in their plan.

Alex caught Hob's eye, and he gave her a quick nod. They'd an important task to do, and it was the first time Simon had entrusted them with this responsibility. They steadied their mounts, dropping to the rear of the group.

Up ahead, Evan gave the silent signal, and like ghostly wraiths, the band of riders and cattle veered sharply right and filed into a narrow gulley hidden behind a huge grey stone.

Jumping off their mounts, Alex and Hob threw their reins to the Stonegarth brothers, grabbed some leafy branches that'd been left beside the stone for just this purpose, and ran back to the track.

Sweeping the branches behind them, they quickly obliterated the hoof-prints and tracks of their band, covering them with fallen autumn leaves.

"Good enough. They won't see that well in the dark," whispered Hob as he stowed his branch and grabbed a larger bough that'd also been left ready beside the stones. "Help me with this."

Alex grasped the branch and together they pulled it into position, then repeated the exercise with several more bushes and limbs until the gulley entrance was invisible from the road.

Just in time! A thunder of hooves came hurtling down from the ford and, like the horsemen of the apocalypse, their Elliot pursuers flew past the hideout, cloaks flapping and lungs straining with their every stride. In their vanguard, a grim-faced rider left a trail of smoke behind him from the smouldering turf atop his lance—the sign that they were on a 'hot trod', a legal pursuit that aimed to catch reivers red-handed and retrieve stolen livestock.

Holding her breath, Alex crouched behind their bushy

screen until their enemies had all passed. Then she stood, stretching muscles that'd cramped after their long ride.

Hob caught her eye and grinned, then they turned to jog along the dry stream bed and join their kinsmen.

Wiry and light-hearted, Hob was a willing compatriot in escapades like this. He was like a brother to her; they'd grown up together, playing together as children, then learning the skills of warfare as they grew. For in the frequently-disputed lands around the frontier between England and Scotland, anyone who was capable of wielding a sword or aiming a bow could be called on at any time to defend their clan or fight for their country, and some of the women were as fierce as their menfolk.

After a short distance Alex and Hob were reunited with the Stonegarth brothers and their horses. Creeping quietly through the wood and along the hidden valley, it wasn't long until they reached the isolated farmhouse that was their destination. Their safe house. Their sanctuary.

~

M ichael pulled his horse to a stop and gaped open-mouthed at the scene in the misty glen before him, his appointment at the assizes in Gretna forgotten. In this remote Scottish valley he hadn't expected to see anyone—or any*thing,* save perhaps a grazing deer or a soaring sparrow-hawk.

Oblivious to the onlooker at the edge of the wood, a slim youth in rough breeches, loose tunic and cloth bonnet sat astride a powerful black stallion on the wide green river meadow.

With signals that were so subtle as to be invisible to Michael's eye, the rider directed the noble beast to prance and leap and spin in such a manner that it appeared to *dance,* although Michael thought himself foolish for such a notion. *How can a horse dance?* But that was what it appeared to be doing—trotting in such a contained manner it reminded him of an Englishman in a gavotte, then spinning on the spot like a fine lady dancing a jig; tail swishing and bit jingling in time with the steps.

What kind of magic is this?

Whatever it was, it struck a chord in Michael's soul; it resonated with things he'd felt in his heart but not known how to express—that riding could be more of an *art* than a mere function; that the horse was capable of being more of a *partner* than a beast of burden or the vehicle of war.

"Sire," he called out and pushed his horse out from under the trees.

At the sound of his voice, the youth froze, and the stallion mirrored his alertness, ready to spin and run at the slightest provocation.

"I mean ye no harm." Michael held up his hands to show he carried no weapon. "But are ye available for hire, lad? I could offer a position at my keep. Would ye consider working for me? I'm laird of Stobs Castle, and I could use someone of your skills to work with my horses." He hesitated, wondering if he was being too honest. "I would wish ye to teach me to ride like that."

"I—I cannot, sire." A tinge of pink crept up the lad's cheek —which, now that Michael was closer and could see him properly, was remarkably smooth.

Michael frowned, and drew his horse alongside so he could study the youth more closely. The horse the lad rode was a fine beast that would've cost a fair penny at the Kelso horse sales. But his clothing spoke of homespun cloth and village markets. In fact, he had the appearance of a servant— apart from his boots, which were made of finest calf leather with brass buckles and the daintiest of heels. *This youth is a contradiction.*

Or possibly a thief?

"Is the horse stolen?" Michael demanded, catching the lad's arm and adding sharply, "Have ye been reiving?"

In this part of the world, cattle rustling was the favoured hobby of most clansmen, and the majority of them weren't above a spot of horse thieving either. And those very reivers —thieving riders—were the reason for Michael's trip to Gretna, on the border between Queen Elizabeth's England and Queen Mary's Scotland.

Once every month or so, the English and Scots wardens met to pass judgement on the wrongdoers of the Scottish and English Marches—the counties that straddled the frontier between two nations that had been at war almost as often as they'd been at peace. The counties that the locals called 'The Borders'. The counties whose inhabitants were usually called Marchmen or Borderers—when they weren't being called reivers.

"No, sir!" the lad gasped. "My father got him for me at Berwick market." His head jerked back defiantly. "And would a stolen horse be trained like *this?*" With this last word, some invisible signal must've passed between them, for the horse spun on its haunches, almost wrenching the youth's arm out of Michael's grip.

But Michael's arms were as strong as the rest of his lean body, from years of hard riding and hard work, and he held fast, dislodging the lad from his saddle and knocking the bonnet from his head.

To Michael's surprise, hanks of long, raven-black hair spilled out of the cloth cap and down the youth's back. "What the—" Without letting go of the arm, Michael jumped off his horse and joined the lad on the ground.

And now that he could see better, it was plainly obvious

that this was no boy. It was a girl—a decidedly pretty one with high cheekbones, full lips and hazel eyes—but disguised in boy's clothing. *How did I ever get that wrong?* "What—*who* are ye, lass?" he asked.

"I might ask the same of you, sire," she replied, her chin tilted and her eyes sparking. "Who are you to accost a lass when she's training her horse? I have me a mind to report you to the warden!"

At this last comment, Michael let out a roar of laughter, releasing the girl's arm as he doubled up with mirth.

"What's so funny?" Her jaw jutted again as she rubbed her arm.

She's a feisty one! "'Tis just—" But he dare not tell a stranger—even one as pretty as this—that he was the deputy warden in this area of Scotland. Others had been killed for less. He shook his head. "No matter. They call me Michael Cranstoun. But I still wait to find out who *you* are, and how ye came to ride so well?"

Righting the stirrup irons, she prepared to mount her horse. "Alexandra Graham."

Michael frowned. He didn't recall the Grahams having a daughter called Alexandra. "Of Ewesdale?"

The girl swung up into the saddle, but didn't answer that question. Instead she answered an earlier one. "I've been reading a book on riding. By an Italian master." From her perch atop the stallion, she looked down at him. "You would do well to find yourself a copy."

She reads? If she could read that definitely meant she was more than a mere servant. *Mayhap the daughter of a laird or someone of high standing.* But how then did he not know of her?

Michael took a hold of the stallion's rein and looked her in the eye. "Next time I ride to Kelso I'll search for it. But until then, would ye teach me? Show me how to make my horse dance like a butterfly on a patch of flowering nettle." He motioned at his grey cob. "I would have him be a willing partner rather than a bonded servant."

Now it was Alexandra's turn to laugh, her shoulders relaxing and her face softening. "You are persistent, sire."

"Meet me here two days from now. At noon?" His business in Gretna should be finished by then, and he'd have time to devote to equestrianism in general. And to this beguiling equestrienne in particular. "Bring an escort, if you wish."

With a tilt of her head and a curl of her lips—but no answer—she turned her horse out of his grasp and trotted away up the glen towards the ford. Towards England.

Michael raised his eyebrows. She might be an accomplished rider, but she had a poor sense of direction, headed as she was—all alone—into enemy country.

With a quick glance at the sun he jumped onto his horse. He would be late for his meeting, but he couldn't be so unchivalrous as to leave a maid alone where robbers might accost her and steal her magnificent horse—or worse.

Setting his spurs into his horse's sides, he raced towards the border in pursuit of the pixie-faced lass who somehow both intrigued and infuriated him in equal measure.

CHAPTER 2

FRIDAY 4TH OCTOBER, 1566

T HAT MAN WOULD *be worth a king's ransom if he got paid by the word.* Michael shifted his feet and regarded the warden of the English East March, who was holding forth at the other side of the large canvas tent that'd been erected to protect the wardens and their officers from the elements.

Sitting proud and stark on the treeless flatlands overlooking the River Esk where it led into the Solway Firth, the seven-foot high granite monolith called Lochmabenstone was one of the southernmost landmarks of the Scottish realm and one of the meeting places used by the wardens on their regular gatherings.

Now that the formal part of the assizes was over, the wardens were making preparations for the next day of truce —the monthly session where English and Scottish wardens would meet to bring criminals to trial.

This month, Sir Walter Ker, Warden of the Scottish Middle March, had been summoned to Edinburgh to advise Queen Mary prior to her upcoming justice eyres in the Borders. So, as his deputy, Michael was attending the warden meeting in Sir Walter's stead; a duty that sat heavily on his shoulders.

The monthly meeting could be a fraught affair. On more than one occasion, a truce day had descended into open hostility, with casualties and even deaths not unknown. So both sides fielded strong-armed bailiffs to control any trouble that might arise after the verdicts had been announced, and watched their words to avoid causing trouble in the first place.

It had been a busy session, the clerk calling forth one complainant after another. In quick succession, the wardens had meted justice for thefts, burnings, kidnappings and raids. But there were no murders to deal with this month, saints be praised.

During the trials, one of Michael's liegemen had been charged with theft, which he vehemently denied. Michael knew Tom Turnbull to be a truthful man and so had obtained Tom's acquittal by attesting to the man's innocence on his own honour as deputy warden.

But taking Tom's offence on his honour would make Michael responsible for the offence if Tom was later found to be guilty. It wasn't the first time he'd spoken for one of his men, and it would likely not be the last. For Michael hated to see injustice win—his desire for balance hard to reconcile with his job as deputy warden, since the raids and counter-raids that the wardens had to mediate were never clear-cut and simple. So he had to do the best he could, dispensing justice as he saw it, being fair-minded to all and biting his tongue, on occasion, to avoid riling the easily-offended English wardens.

One of those, the earl of Bedford, was a commanding figure with a paunch that spoke of an overindulgence of mutton, abundant grey whiskers, a long straight nose—and a voice that droned like a bee in clover.

A voice that might've sent Michael to sleep—like old Lord Home, Warden of the Scottish East March, who slumped quietly on a camp stool in the far corner. But Michael couldn't sleep, for his thoughts kept turning to the elusive lass he'd met that morning. The lass he was beginning to think might be one of the wee folk.

For when he rode over the border into Kershope Glen to rescue the fair maid who had inadvertently strayed into England, sword at the ready and senses on high alert, there was no sign of her—just the burbling stream, a light breeze rustling the trees and the weak October sun dappling everything in shades of russet and saffron. Alexandra had disappeared, as if she'd been stolen by the faeries—or as if she'd been merely a figment of his imagination.

Michael was brought back to the present when something the pompous English warden said caught his attention.

"'Tis my belief," the earl smoothed his moustache with gold-ringed fingers, "that these outlaw Armstrongs must be taken in-hand. 'Tis said they can put three thousand men into saddle and that they are the most feared and dangerous riding clan in the whole of the Marches." He swept a velvet-covered arm around the gathering. "They mustn't be allowed to flaunt justice like this. If Cecil hears of it, he'll get Elizabeth to send her army, and we will have open warfare. Another war!"

At this last comment, Sir John Maxwell, long-serving warden of the Scottish West March, intervened. "My Lord, we cannot have that! Our kinsfolk have had warring armies plundering our herds and our crops for centuries. There's not a farm or village in the Scottish Borders that hasn't suffered over the years."

His deputy chimed in. "Yes! We may live on the border, but we deserve better than to be an unwilling supply wagon for every English king—or queen—with designs on Scotland!"

Lord Scrope raised a sardonic eyebrow. "Not just English kings. You Scots have sent your fair number of armies into England too."

"That is exactly what concerns me," said the earl. "These Armstrongs are strong enough to field an army all by themselves."

"And Carlisle is but a short march over the border," added Lord Scrope—who, as well as being warden of the English West March, was also governor of Carlisle. Almost to himself, he added, "I must ask Elizabeth for reinforcements."

Seeing that the discussion was in danger of getting out of hand, Michael raised his voice. "Gentlemen, I urge ye to remember why we're here. If we look at this impartially, *both* sides of the border have suffered greatly in times of war. And both sides of the border suffer by the Armstrongs—they not only reive into England, they also steal from us Scots."

He inclined his head at Bedford. "But I agree with the earl. Something needs to be done about them. Here's what I suggest." At this, all the men present turned towards him— even old Home, who had awoken at all the rumpus. "We expect Mary, our queen, to arrive at Jedburgh any day now, where she will hold justice eyres. I propose that I return and make representation to her, asking for a show of force to deal with the Armstrong troublemakers."

Lord Home coughed into his kerchief and then flapped it in Michael's direction. "Good idea, young man. Go and speak to her." He wiped his mouth. "Tell her I said we need to quash these ruffians before they cause a war."

If I wish to keep my head, I'll 'tell' the queen nothing, Michael thought, but kept his face straight. "I will ask that of Her Grace."

He turned to Bedford and the other wardens. "My Lords,

will that satisfy? I'll impress upon the queen of our concerns and ask for a speedy resolution. At our next meeting I'll provide an update." *And it'll be my job to make the queen understand the gravity of the situation, before Scrope and the Armstrongs pitch us into another war.*

A shiver ran down his spine at that thought, for every Borderer was brought up on stories of Flodden field. Flodden, the remote Cheviot hillside where the Scottish army was routed by the English, losing its king and the flower of its chivalry, decimating every family in the Borders for years afterwards and causing political upheaval that took decades to resolve.

It was not the only occasion in the turbulent history of the Borders where the English and the Scots had met in mortal combat, but it was the bloodiest, and Michael had no wish to see a battle like that repeated in his lifetime.

∿

"My thanks, Sir Walter." Mary Stuart, Queen of Scots, inclined her head so the old warden would know he was dismissed. "I 'ad not realised the situation in the Marches was so serious. You 'ave given me much to think on. But I will keep you no longer."

"Your Grace." Sir Walter Ker bowed stiffly, using the traditional Scots form of address for royalty. A thickset man with a drooping white moustache, Sir Walter was warden of the Scottish Middle March, summoned to advise the queen before her forthcoming visit to the Borders. But the news he brought had chilled her heart.

With a flourish of his deep-green cape, Ker took his leave, exiting the tapestried drawing room, a page pushing the heavy oaken door closed behind him.

Mary moved to the window, pushed aside the heavy

drapes, and gazed over the parkland adjacent to Holyrood Palace. Under the lumpen hill the locals called Arthur's Seat, after the mythical Celtic king, the grassy parkland of the palace grounds lured her. On a different day, she'd have sent for her white palfrey and gone for a gallop, hoping to forget her worries and enjoy the crisp autumn air.

But Sir Walter's stories of the wild men of the Borders and their marauding ways had convinced her that her realm was in danger. She needed to take action, and without delay. She needed a *man* of action, a man who would not question her orders or fail to deliver a result.

And it took little thought to realise that she knew just the man for the job.

James Hepburn.

Strong, daring, loyal, and a skilled military man, he and his band of mosstroopers would soon bring those Liddesdale reivers to heel and deliver peace to the Borders. He even had a castle right on their doorstep. *Oui. He will do it.*

Calling her page over, she delivered her instructions. "Go fetch Lord Bothwell. Tell 'im I 'ave an important task for 'im."

CHAPTER 3

"**R**IDE!" AT THE head of his company of three hundred fierce horsemen, James Hepburn, Earl of Bothwell, stood in his stirrups and pointed his lance. "To Liddesdale!"

The clatter of trotting hooves bounced off stone walls and echoed around the narrow closes of Edinburgh's Royal Mile as Bothwell's troop left Edinburgh Castle, heading south to the Borders. Aboard their sturdy hobblers, the fighting men bristled with arms and machismo, sending clouds of pigeons into the sky and causing the goodwives of Edinburgh to scuttle into the safety of their homes.

As he passed Holyrood and pointed his horse south, Bothwell looked up at the palace, wondering if the queen would be watching from one of the many mullioned windows. Sitting taller in the saddle, he straightened his shield and thrust out his chest, hoping the sun would glint off his breastplate and cause him to look like a knight of old. He'd even chosen this grey cob—narrow-girthed enough to make his short legs seem longer, and white to give the illusion of purity—to deliberately promote that image. For he wanted to persuade the queen that he, James Hepburn, could be the strong champion she needed to protect her realm. And her sovereignty.

For now, the queen's bastard half-brother Moray might hold sway as her prime minister. But Bothwell's plan to usurp the dour-faced, emotionless turncoat was gaining momentum, and this latest commission would give him the perfect opportunity to prove his worth to the queen.

Once he'd flung those Armstrong curs into the dungeons of Hermitage Castle, their fates would be sealed. And his would be on the ascendence.

A shaft of sunlight peeked round the cliffs of Salisbury Crags and bathed Bothwell in its warmth. *A good omen*, he thought with a grim smile, imagining the imposing figure he must present to onlookers and adversaries alike.

He would get Liddesdale under control, drag those vile reivers to Jedburgh so the queen could hang them, and ensure that Mary realised it was *he*, James Hepburn, Chief Lieutenant of the Scottish Marches, who was responsible for bringing peace to the turbulent Borders. She would soon realise that if he could master the unruly reivers, he could also help tame her rebellious Protestant lords—and then the English throne.

At that thought, his heart leaped in his chest. But then he cautioned himself. *One step at a time.* He must defeat the Armstrongs first; only then could he set his sights higher. And he meant to rise higher.

Right to the very top.

For what queen could resist a champion who would unquestioningly stamp on her enemies, promote her cause and bring peace to her land? James Hepburn, Earl of Bothwell, Lord High Admiral of Scotland, and Duke of Orkney, would be that man, and he would happily destroy any opponent who stood in his way. Or hers. He would be the queen's man—whatever it took.

~

Michael rode away from Lochmabenstone, the sun sending its orange rays over the shallow waters of the Solway Firth. A cool wind sighed over the mudflats and a fan of black crows filled the air, their harsh calls discordant as they returned to their roosts. His mind whirling, he wrapped his cloak tighter around his shoulders and urged his horse into a trot, undecided on the best course of action.

For he needed to get to Jedburgh with utmost haste—on the morrow, if he could—to petition the queen about the Armstrongs and ensure that the English had no excuse to invade the Scottish Marches.

But he also had a tryst tomorrow with the mysterious Alexandra—a tryst which *she* mightn't keep, but if he himself didn't keep the appointment, he would never know. And she'd intrigued him sufficiently that he needed to at least *try* and see her again. For her mischievous smile and green-flecked eyes danced at the forefront of his thoughts like an elusive will o' the wisp.

How could he keep both appointments?

I'll just have to ride hard, he thought, *meet Alexandra at Kershopefoot then travel on to Stobs and pick up a fresh horse*. If he left the castle at first light he could get to Jedburgh early the following day, where, if the saints were with him, he would be in time to meet with the Stuart queen and prevent another war.

Decision made, he pointed his horse towards the inn at Gretna where he'd booked lodging for the night. A hearty meal and a good night's rest would give him energy for the day to come. For he had a feeling he would need *all* of his energy—and more—over the next four and twenty hours.

CHAPTER 4

SATURDAY 5TH OCTOBER, 1566

ALEX TIGHTENED THE muscles of her stomach, steadying Duke's canter. But he felt like a fiery cauldron underneath her today, as if he might boil over at any moment, his muscles coiled and his ears pricked. She grinned. This power was good, as long as she could contain it and use it to her advantage. If not, she could end up unceremoniously dumped on the ground with a long walk home and a dent to more than her pride!

'Twill be my fault he's flighty today. Duke picked up on her mood and feelings, and however much she tried to ignore it, Alex couldn't deny the tingle of anticipation or hastening of her pulse every time she thought of the strange rider who had accosted her the other day.

Michael. She even liked his name. She'd warmed to him, even though he was a Scot and should've been her sworn enemy. But there was something about him—an air of calm, so different from her own fiery nature; a sense that he had hidden strengths to complement the powerful muscles that'd been so obvious when he pulled her off her horse.

19

She'd forgiven him for that, because he seemed to genuinely *want* to learn to ride better. And because—who could *not* forgive a man with hair the colour of burnished gold and eyes that gleamed carnelian blue with eyelashes so long they could've graced a maid...

Stop thinking of him! Alex pulled Duke to a halt and squinted at the sun, mired as it was behind banks of grey cloud. She frowned. It was after noon, and she had achieved nothing in her training session for she was letting her imagination get in the way—indulging herself with fanciful notions of a man she'd met for mere moments, who had obviously not remembered the assignation he'd made with her.

Squaring her shoulders, she turned Duke's head northwards up the valley and urged him into a gallop. Hooves pounding, nostrils flaring and mane streaming, the black stallion raced up the springy turf beside the wide stream.

The wind in Alex's eyes caused tears to run down her cheeks, but she dashed them away. For it was past time for their meet, and a headlong sprint on a willing steed was the best way she knew to clear her head. It seemed that Michael had indeed forgotten about her, so she must likewise forget about him, hard as it might be.

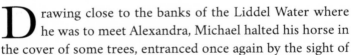

Drawing close to the banks of the Liddel Water where he was to meet Alexandra, Michael halted his horse in the cover of some trees, entranced once again by the sight of the girl on her black stallion.

She has come! He breathed a sigh of relief. After all his doubts and worries, here she was once more, still wearing her boyish cap and rough clothes, the stallion displaying his quality and presence, even at a distance.

Today, however, the pair looked less like dancers and more like warriors about to charge into battle, with a pent-up energy that pervaded every move. It was a spellbinding sight, more so now that he knew that those long legs which wrapped so lithely around the horse's sides belonged to a rather lovely lass, rather than a scruffy youth.

And she's alone. He didn't know whether to feel pleased or offended by that. For the lack of an escort implied that she didn't see him as a manly threat to her propriety. But it also meant that it would be easier for them to talk without hindrance.

With a smile playing on his lips, he pushed his horse forward—just as Alexandra turned her mount up the valley and raced off at a flat-out gallop.

For a heartbeat, Michael hesitated—and then he too flew up the river meadow, chasing after this elusive woman who sat a horse better than any man he'd ever known.

Her horse is fast, too. Mist, Michael's poor beast, had already travelled sixteen miles that morning, since leaving the lodging at Gretna, and was carrying a heavier load. It was an unequal race. *I may have to content myself with catching her once she stops.* For the black stallion ran as if the very hounds of hell were chasing him, his tail streaming behind him like a lure, and the rider on his back crouched low over his neck as if to protect herself from the wind.

Somehow, she must've sensed Michael's presence—or heard the heaving lungs of his straining horse as Mist struggled to close the distance between them. Looking over her shoulder, Alexandra's eyes widened when she spied the grey horse and his rider following in her wake.

It seemed for a moment that she checked her stallion as if to slow him, for his stride changed—and that was her undoing. The black stumbled on a hidden ditch, sending his rider flying over his head and tumbling onto the ground ahead.

Heart in his mouth, Michael closed the distance between them at breakneck speed, praying under his breath to Mary and all the saints.

For Alexandra lay pale and unmoving, and Michael feared the worst.

CHAPTER 5

A S IF FROM a great distance, Alex heard the deep rumble of a man's voice. What he was saying, she couldn't tell, but his tone spoke of uncertainty and worry.

Someone was pounding a sledgehammer in her head, and her eyelids felt like they were made of lead, but with a great effort of will, she forced her eyes to open. And then shut them almost as quickly. *It's so bright.*

But the man's voice took on a more hopeful note, and his words began to unscramble. "Alexandra," he was saying. "Wake up!"

Opening her eyes again, she blinked hard as the grey light assailed her senses. Then the face of a viking blotted out the sky. A viking in a deep-blue doublet. At this nonsensical vision she began to shake her head—but that hurt too.

Under her hands she could feel grass—and it was damp. *Why am I lying on the ground?* She made to sit up, which was when she discovered that her left arm hurt even more than her head.

As the arm gave way, she would've collapsed back on the

ground, but the man—*Michael*, she remembered now—caught her and eased her into a sitting position.

"How d'ye feel?" he asked, concern sparking in his eyes. Kneeling beside her, he steadied her against his chest. Even in her stupor, she couldn't help but notice how wide and strong he was. This wasn't a man who spent his days indoors playing courtly intrigues.

She took a deep breath and cradled her injured arm, tucking it safely under her breasts. "What happened?" she asked, surprised at how feeble her voice sounded.

"You had a fall," he answered—and then she remembered.

"Duke!" she cried, scanning the area around them frantically.

Michael motioned over his shoulder. "He's fine—he's grazing over there with my beast." He raised an eyebrow. "A gelding, fortunately. If mine had been a mare, they mayn't have been quite so quiet..."

Alex laughed, even though it hurt. *He has a sense of humour.* And he was no prude, like many of the English nobles she'd met. "Are all Scots men like you?" she asked, then clapped her good hand over her mouth. "Forgive me! I didn't mean to be impolite."

With a chuckle, he motioned at their position. "I think I may be the only man in Scotland right now who is kneeling on the damp earth with a pretty lass in his arms. So no, I suppose there aren't many like me."

He didn't seem to have noticed her slip of the tongue, where she'd said 'Scots men' rather than just 'men', inferring that she was English. Maybe he thought she was still discomposed. For if he knew who she *really* was, he mightn't ever speak to her again. And that, she was realising, would make her sad. Very sad indeed.

∾

"Let me bind your arm," Michael said, and Alex thought she might faint all over again.

For he unbuttoned his doublet and pulled off his shirt, revealing the lean, well-muscled frame that she'd been sure lay beneath his courtly appearance. Powerful shoulders with rippling muscles lay above a wide chest that made her pulse beat harder.

"Here," he ripped the arms off his shirt and tied the cuffs together, then passed the length of white cotton around her back. "Tell me if it hurts," he added as he fastened the ends together over her elbow.

"No, 'tis fine," she said, testing the binding. It hurt less, now that he'd tied her arm to her body.

"'Tis the bone here—" he pointed at the long bone below her neck, "that's broken, not your arm. But immobilising your arm will make it less painful."

"How d'you know all this? Are you a physician?" she asked, and then wondered again if she'd been too forward.

Pulling the remnants of his shirt back over his head and hiding that magnificent chest, much to her disappointment, he chuckled. "'Tis a long story, which I shall tell you some day when you're not lying injured in the middle of Armstrong territory."

Alex caught the inference of his words—that they might meet again—and was contemplating whether he might really *mean* it, when he let out a low groan.

"I *knew* I shouldn't have mentioned those ruffians," he said, grabbing her round the waist and pulling her to her feet.

A mile or two away—but moving fast—a dark smudge that could only be a large band of riders moved towards them, down the wide meadows of the Liddel valley.

Reivers, almost certainly. Armstrongs most likely. The

worst and most infamous clan of reivers, who would think nothing of murdering two unlucky travellers solely for the prize of their two horses and whatever they carried in their saddlebags.

"We need to get out of here," Michael added. Unnecessarily.

~

Alex hobbled towards Duke. "Help me onto my horse," she gasped, but Michael was one step ahead of her.

Pulling his grey behind him, he lifted her onto Duke as if she weighed no more than a child, then leapt up behind her. One arm circled her waist to steady her, the other hand held both sets of reins as he wheeled the horses round.

"Careful!" Alex cautioned. "Duke is used to subtle signals. Let me guide him—I don't need the reins."

Michael seemed about to protest, but then thought better of it. "D'you know somewhere we can hide?"

"Yes," she said, urging Duke forward as the dust cloud behind them grew larger. "Make sure your horse keeps up."

~

Galloping back along the banks of the Liddel Water, Alex ignored the pounding in her head, scanning anxiously ahead for the small stone cairns that denoted the ford.

Behind them, she was sure the sounds of galloping hooves were getting louder, and she gritted her teeth and knotted her good hand into Duke's mane.

Time seemed to slow, as if she and Michael were running through a mire and the band of riders behind them were on the normal clock, gaining on them with every yard.

Finally, when she'd almost given up hope, and the reivers were too close for comfort, she spotted the ford. "Steady," she called, sitting taller in the saddle and slowing Duke to a trot.

Michael swore as he was nearly pulled out of the saddle by his grey, who ran riderless beside them but hadn't decelerated as sharply as Duke.

"Sorry," she said. "We turn left here. Over the ford."

"But that is into England!" Michael protested, pulling on Duke's reins so harshly that the horse threw his head up in protest, skidding to a halt.

She caught his eye over her shoulder. "Trust me! And let *me* ride." Nudging Duke with her heels, he marched forward into the shallows. "We shall escape them yet."

But her words rang hollow when a blood-curdling yell behind them showed that they'd been spotted, and that the chase was on!

CHAPTER 6

ONE LOOK FROM those amazing hazel eyes—and one war-cry from the approaching reivers—was enough to convince Michael. "As you wish," he said, and clicked his tongue to encourage the grey forward.

Moments later they'd splashed through the ford and were cantering through the trees along the Kershope valley. Michael glanced over his shoulder, but there was no sign—yet—of their pursuers. "Where now?" he whispered into Alexandra's ear, uncomfortably aware of how close and how warm her body was, but also uncomfortably aware that they were running headlong into English territory.

"Trust me," she said again, scanning the right-hand side of the path, "and be ready to dismount when I say."

Up ahead, the trees thickened and the undergrowth beside the track became less sparse, with elder and wild garlic vying with ivy and blackthorn for space under the towering oaks, gnarly rowans or silvery birch trees of the ancient wood.

They'd gone but a few hundred yards further when Alexandra stiffened and called out again, "Steady!"

As if by magic, the stallion slowed to a walk. "Quickly," she said, "jump off and lead your horse behind me in single file. Make no sound."

He raised his eyebrows at her commanding tone—uselessly, since she was before him and couldn't see his face—but did as she requested.

Turning the stallion sharp right off the track, she rode him at a large stone—and disappeared!

I knew she was a witch! But Michael's horse was hot on the heels of the stallion, and all of a sudden they too had disappeared around the granite monolith, which hid the entrance to a dry stream bed.

"Throw me your reins," Alex hissed at him from atop the black, crouching low over his neck so that she wouldn't be seen from the track, her face pale in the dim light of the forest, "and use a branch to hide our tracks."

Her added admonition of "Quickly!" was unnecessary, for Michael was already hurrying back around the stone and brushing frantically at their hoof-prints, conscious of the approaching thunder of their pursuers, who must by now have crossed the ford and be very close behind.

~

C rouching together behind the grey stone as the reivers charged along the Kershope track and on up the valley, Michael's heart pounded loudly against his ribcage. He was unsure whether the blood coursed through his veins from fear, the thrill of the chase, or the fact that Alexandra was in his arms once more. Her good side held safely against his chest, his arm circled her waist from when he'd pulled her off her horse.

Even after the Armstrongs—for it *was* them, he recognised the red-bearded Dod Armstrong in the lead—had passed, her right arm remained wrapped round his shoulders.

It brought her face to a level with his own and made him uncomfortably aware of the rise and fall of her chest under the thin tunic she wore, and the tumble of dark hair that framed her head like a halo, for she'd lost the cloth cap when she fell. He swallowed. She was captivating, and each minute that he spent in her company she intrigued and beguiled him even more.

"Thank you," she breathed, turning her face towards him, eyes wide, cheeks flushed and lips full.

In that moment, he could resist her no longer.

Leaning against the grey granite, he bent his head and his mouth sought hers. Her lips were soft as rose petals in summer, her skin fragrant like vanilla, and, to his surprise, she tasted sweet, like honey from a comb. Surely he would drown in the loveliness of her.

Her yelp as he pulled her closer, pinning her injured arm in its makeshift sling between them, brought him to his senses.

What am I doing, kissing this maid here in enemy territory when the Armstrongs are abroad and might descend on us at any moment?

He broke their embrace, breathing heavily. "Forgive me."

Alex's skin tingled, every nerve-ending singing and her pulse racing. The misgivings she'd harboured about Michael such a short time ago seemed laughable now, with his arms encircling her body and his lips bewitching her senses. With his mouth on hers, she forgot the pounding in her temples and the ache from her shoulder. He made her forget her very self.

Alex had never felt like this before.

Yes, she'd shared curious kisses with a couple of the boys from her clan; but *this!* This was something beyond all imagining. How could he do these things to her? It was like some sort of magic.

"Forgive me," he panted, pushing her to arm's length.

She almost cried, wanting more of his embrace; wanting that feeling to never stop.

"We should seek safety. The Armstrongs will return once they realise they've lost us. And my breath comes so hard even a deaf man could hear me! My most humble apologies for taking advantage of you," he gave her a half-bow—as much as he could while still partially supporting her, for her legs wouldn't hold her up, "'Twas unforgivable of me, lass, even in the heat of the moment. It wilna happen again."

Her spirits plummeted, and tears pricked at the corners of her eyes. Her head whirled. *He doesn't want me. It was just the excitement of the chase.* She turned away so he wouldn't see her tears, and quickly wiped her cheek with her uninjured hand.

"This way," she said, jerking her chin in the direction of the farmhouse. But her legs were still weak from the tumble, and her head dizzy—whether from his kiss or the fall she was unsure—and her knees turned to water even as she made to grab Duke's reins.

Darkness roared in from the edges of her vision, robbing her of sight and senses so that the last thing she saw was Duke's noble face, before the shadows took over and everything went black.

CHAPTER 7

MICHAEL PAUSED AT the edge of the wood and surveyed the secret place before him.

Tucked away in this hidden fold of land, the bastle house with its camouflaged approach was the perfect location to escape the ravages of reiver country. Surrounded by a drystane dyke, with just one gate for entry, the fortified farmhouse with its thick stone walls and arrow-slit windows was constructed to repel all but the most determined attack—if any enemy would ever find it. The upper-level living with its removable access ladder was designed to keep the inhabitants safe and warm above the ground-level barn below, which housed their most valuable stock. But would this house keep Alexandra safe? And would *he*, as a Scotsman, be safe to approach it?

Looking down at the girl he carried in his arms, his heart wrenched. She'd fainted again after the trauma of their chase and the romantic tryst they'd enjoyed. But this time she hadn't awoken, and he was desperately worried.

Glancing over his shoulder, and past the two horses that followed behind, he chewed his lip. He hadn't heard the

Armstrongs return—yet—but he was sure they would be tearing the woods apart, hunting high and low for Alexandra's valuable stallion, if nothing else.

What he faced was like a choice between the hangman's noose and the executioner's sword: Scottish cutthroats or enemy English farmers? But when he thought of it like that, farmers seemed considerably less dangerous than Armstrongs. Even if they *were* English.

Maybe he could pretend to be one of their countrymen? He could say he was from clan Hall. They were prevalent in the East March, on both sides of the border—and far enough away from here that he shouldn't be called out on his subterfuge.

Squaring his shoulders, he pulled Alexandra tighter against his chest and stepped out of the shelter of the trees, towards the wooden gate.

~

"Halt!" called a gruff voice before Michael had walked more than a dozen paces. "Who are you, and what's your business here?"

Lifting the unconscious Alexandra higher in his arms to show to the shadowy figure in the first-floor doorway, Michael shouted back, "Michael Hall, sire. I found this injured lass up the valley there." He nodded over his shoulder at her horse. "She fell from her horse. And there are Armstrongs abroad."

At this last statement the man in the doorway stiffened, then dropped a wooden ladder from his perch down to the ground. "You'd better come up then. Leave the horses down below. Hob will attend to them."

The door to the barn below opened, and a youth with a shock of red hair and dressed in a similar fashion to

Alexandra darted out. "Alex!" he cried when he spotted the girl, and looked up at Michael. "What happened to her?"

He knows her? Now it was Michael's turn to freeze. *She called herself Alexandra Graham.* But like the Halls, there were Grahams on both sides of the border. Had the girl hoodwinked him? Was she indeed *English*, not Scots as he'd assumed?

That put a whole different complexion on things. Could she be a spy, playing him for a fool, or were her agreeable nature and obvious charms for real?

Michael looked down at the maid in his arms and gritted his teeth. Emotions in disarray after the intensity of their embrace, his usual level-headed reasoning was proving elusive. *I'll think on it later. For now, I need to get away from this enemy stronghold, elude the Armstrongs, ride on to Stobs before nightfall, and then to Jedburgh and the queen.* He had more than enough problems to deal with without letting his feelings get in the way.

"Fell off her horse. We need to get her inside." Michael handed the horses' reins to the boy and stepped round to the ladder.

With her injury, this will be awkward. "Sorry," he muttered, even though he knew she wouldn't hear, then lifted her over his shoulder to leave a hand free for the climb.

Taking a deep breath, and hoping he wasn't climbing to his death, he stepped onto the first rung.

CHAPTER 8

TROTTING ALONG AT the head of his victorious troops, Bothwell allowed himself a self-satisfied smile. His plan had started well, with the defeat of Whithaugh Tower and the capture of three-score Armstrongs, including their leader, Archie o' the Bell.

Next on his list were the Armstrongs of Mangerton, their accomplices the Elliots of Shaws, and then the Elliots of Park. Those should fill his dungeons nicely and keep Queen Mary's gibbets in Jedburgh full for a week or more. More to the point, the capture of all those notorious ruffians would send a message to the other riding families of the Borders: that they needed to toe the line or they would have the wrath of Bothwell land upon them.

Crossing Hermitage Water, Bothwell turned his horse towards the impregnable castle that had been in his family for nearly a century. Hermitage was not the most comfortable place to live, with its large, cold rooms and arrow-slit windows, but its imposing grandeur warmed his heart and bolstered his pride. For who would dare oppose him when he stood behind those unassailable walls?

Answering the sentry's challenge with a raise of a round shield emblazoned with the lion-rampant of Scotland, Bothwell led his men under the castle's high stone ramparts and round to the main entrance.

"Fling them into the pit," he ordered, striding up the stairs to his apartments in the Douglas Tower. "Let's see if a few days in the dark will incline them towards truth when they meet their queen." *Or their maker*, he thought with satisfaction. For ruffians like these deserved nothing except the rough justice they would receive at the end of a hangman's noose, and he meant to be the one to deliver them to the assizes where they would meet their end.

~

I nside the bastle house there were more people than Michael would've imagined, and he had to forcibly stop his hand from touching the hilt of his weapon for reassurance. Any movement like that could be seen as hostile in a room full of strangers.

By the door, the man with the gruff voice took one glance at the injured girl and pointed to a wooden bed in the corner. "Set her on the cot over there." He held out a large hand, eyes cold as steel. "And give me your sword for safe-keeping."

Michael did as he asked, laying Alexandra carefully on the straw mattress and handing over his weapon. He felt naked without it. But not so naked as he'd have felt if they'd also asked for the dirk that was hidden in his boot. *But pray that I dinna need to defend myself.* For he was more than outnumbered now, and the dagger would do little against angry enemies armed with longswords.

In the shadows by the arrow-slit windows he could see two sentries, one to the east and one to the west. Round a sturdy wooden table sat a group of burly men, saying little but staring suspiciously at the newcomer. Wavering light from large candles cast pools of brightness into the gloom, and at the far end of the large room, a matronly woman stood by the stone fireplace, tending a large metal pot.

When she spotted Alexandra she set down her spoon and hurried over, wiping her hands on her apron. "What's happened to my wee lamb?"

Michael didn't think the strong-minded Alexandra would appreciate being called a lamb, but he kept that thought to himself. "She fell from her horse. 'Tis my thought that she's broken the long bone at her collar. But she swooned some minutes back and hasnae woken. Mayhap she's injured her head also."

The older woman fetched some cold water and pressed a damp cloth to Alexandra's forehead, at which point the gruff leader strode over and confronted Michael.

"Michael Hall, you say? What's your business here?"

A naturally honest man, Michael had always found that if the whole truth couldn't be told, stories as close to the facts as possible were easiest remembered. And easiest defended. "I've a message from the wardens of the Marches to take to the Scots queen, Mary Stuart, at Jedburgh." Michael stood taller. "And who be you, to question the queen's messenger so?"

The man narrowed his eyes, but answered. "Simon Graham, Lord of Kersdale and master of this keep. How came you by the lass?"

If this large man with the craggy face knew how good a rider Alexandra was, he wouldn't believe that she'd merely fallen from her mount.

Again, Michael told the truth. Just not all of it. "Her horse took a tumble and she was thrown to the ground. I was on my way up the valley and came to her aid. I bound her arm," he pointed at the makeshift sling, "and was helping her onto her horse when we spotted a band of reivers in the distance. So she showed me the hiding place behind the grey stone, and we hid from the Armstrongs. We were heading here for safety when she fainted."

For a full minute, The Graham regarded Michael, unsmiling and unspeaking.

Michael resisted the temptation to speak into the silence, standing tall and proud instead, as befitted a messenger to the queen.

It was the old woman who broke the impasse, renewing the cold compress on Alexandra's head and provoking a moan from the injured girl. "Alex, dearie, can you hear me?" she crooned, taking the lass's hand.

Michael's heart lightened. At least Alexandra was recovering, even if she *had* led him to an enemy stronghold.

"What...where...where am I?" she mumbled, her eyelids flickering but remaining closed.

"Home, dearie. All safe now." The old woman patted Alexandra's hand.

Alexandra blinked several times, then her eyes opened fully and fastened on Michael's. At first her gaze was blank, showing no recognition. And then a pink tinge crept into her cheeks and her eyes spun away.

Aye, she remembers me. Mayhap she remembered their kiss also. Or perhaps it was guilt at some deception? Michael clenched his jaw and resolved to get to the bottom of this—if he could somehow manage to talk his way out of this English enclave.

~

Seeing his daughter now recovered, Simon Graham seemed to reach a decision. Striding to the doorway, he picked up a sword.

Alex's throat went dry, and her heart began to hammer in her chest.

"I'm grateful for your aid to my daughter," her father said, turning back to Michael, his face hard. "But you are a Scot. And now you know the whereabouts of our safe house, which is a secret from all, save my family and servants." He pulled the weapon from its scabbard then tested its edge with the ball of his thumb. "We can't risk its whereabouts being made known. Peter!" He jerked his chin at a small, solidly-built man with more hair on his chin than his head. "Tie him up and take him outside!"

Standing just a few steps away from Alex's bed, Michael's face turned pale and he tensed, balling his hands into fists, the muscles of his shoulders bunching into knots.

What've I got him into? I must stop this. Despite the ache in her shoulder, Alex pushed herself upright. "Father!" Her voice was higher-pitched then normal and cut through the hubbub in the room. "Have you no mercy? This man saved my life. How can you think to harm him?"

Her father shook his head decisively. "We can't allow him to go free. He could bring great danger to us all!"

"Well, keep him here then. As a prisoner. But don't repay his kindness to your only daughter with barbarity. He could've saved himself and left me to the Armstrongs, but instead he risked his life to save me!" It still felt like someone was banging a drum behind Alex's temples, but she gritted her teeth and ignored the pain. This was more important.

Dark eyebrows knitted over Simon's grey eyes as he regarded his daughter, and a muscle twitched in his jaw.

Good. He's weakening. She tried a different tactic. "We could make him swear an oath. On the life of his queen. Or his God?"

Her father grunted, then swung the sword he carried in a low arc.

Alex's heart stopped.

But Simon merely waved the weapon in his bondman's direction. "Peter, tie him to one of the posts in the barn." He dug the point of the sword into the floor and leaned the heels of his hands on its hilt.

Alex let out a silent breath and glanced quickly at Michael from under her lashes.

His shoulders had visibly relaxed, and he gave her an imperceptible nod, before holding his wrists out for Peter to bind them.

As Michael was led out by Peter, and down the ladder, her father's gruff voice followed them down. "Tell Hob to keep an eye on him. And you can take first watch tonight."

CHAPTER 9

MICHAEL AWOKE FROM a fitful sleep with a start, every muscle in his body tensed at the feel of the warm hand covering his mouth. It exerted enough pressure to prevent him crying out. *Has Lord Kersdale come to finish me off?*

Struggling against the bonds that held him, Michael writhed and twisted, trying to free himself from the constricting hand. But his captors had tied him tightly, and he had little range of movement. Otherwise he might've been free before now.

The shadow in front of him moved, and the weak moonlight filtering through the narrow window-slits high in the thick barn walls illuminated the contours of a profile he well recognised. *Alexandra!* He stopped struggling.

Slowly removing the hand from his mouth, she raised a finger to her lips, then a glint of light caught the edge of a dagger as she moved to work one-handedly on his bonds, her injured arm still bound at her waist.

A minute later he was free, rubbing his wrists to restore the feeling, and walking carefully on feet that were so numb they felt three sizes bigger than normal. Creeping behind Alexandra across the darkness of the barn, he passed warm shapes that munched contentedly on piles of hay, breath steaming slightly in the muggy air. The barn wasn't the most fragrant place he'd ever been, and he was glad when they reached the door and fresh air—stepping over the motionless body of Peter Forster as they did so.

Outside, all was peaceful; the sky cloudless and the half-moon riding high in the infinite blackness of the firmament, stars scattered like diamond dust on dark velvet, a light wind soughing through the shadowy trees edging the hidden bowl they were in.

Taking deep—quiet—breaths of the blessedly clean air, Michael touched Alexandra's arm and gestured enquiringly at Peter's prone form.

She mimed sleep and then a blow to the head.

Michael raised his eyebrows. *I must remember me to not get on the wrong side of this one.*

Alexandra leaned over to pick something up, then hurried across the enclosure, stopping beside a grazing horse that gleamed silver in the moonlight. *Mist.* Slipping a bridle over the gelding's head, she threw Michael some pieces of sacking and lengths of rope, pointing at the horse's feet. A job that would need two hands.

Heart in his mouth lest someone hear them, Michael bound the canvas round Mist's hooves then led the horse to the gate, its steps muffled, following Alexandra.

With a wary glance back at the quiet bastle house, Alexandra unlatched the gate. The faintest of clinks seemed magnified in the noiseless dark, and they both froze.

But there was no movement or shout of alarm from the farmhouse, and after a heart-stopping minute Michael risked a quiet breath before following Alexandra through the gate.

Only once they were some distance away, moving

stealthily up the hidden valley, did Michael dare speak. He caught up with Alexandra and took her free hand, pulling her to a stop. "Thank you, lassie," he whispered. "But you shouldn't have risked yourself for me."

Eyes shining bright, she tilted her head towards him, biting back a smile. "Likewise."

He smiled ruefully. She had him there. "What—"

She put a finger to his lips. "Later," she mouthed, and beckoned him forwards, leading him the remaining distance to the shadowy stone, which gleamed dully in the light of the waxing moon, the flecks of silvery mica bound within the granite reflecting glimmers of pale moonshine filtering through the canopy of trees.

With a few steps they were around the monolith and onto the Kershope track, facing towards Scotland. Michael's heart lightened at the thought of his native land, although he knew they were not yet out of danger. At any time, they could be stumbled on by marauding reivers, or the Grahams could awaken and notice the missing prisoner. But at least now, thanks to Alexandra's brave rescue, he had a chance of making it back to Stobs, and then on to Jedburgh to meet with the queen.

Alexandra halted and pointed at Mist. "You should ride now," she said, her voice low, "and make your escape. I am only sorry I couldn't retrieve your saddle to make the journey more comfortable."

"No matter," Michael said, leaping onto Mist's wide back, "I can manage bareback." He held out an arm to her. "Ride with me?"

She held his eye for a moment, then took his proffered hand and jumped up behind him. "Only to the border," she said, "then I must return and cover our tracks." She wrapped her good arm around his waist.

Michael nodded and urged Mist forward.

He'd forgotten how good it felt to have her next to him, with the faintest scent of vanilla and the tantalising warmth of her body. Distracting thoughts filled his brain as Mist plodded up the drove road and it seemed only seconds until they pulled up at the edge of the woods, facing out on the wide Liddesdale glen.

Tinted grey in the moonlight, the flat bottom of the vale was covered with scrubby grass as far as the eye could see, dotted with the occasional black rock or mossy tussock and fringed by the dark shapes of the glowering hills and forests beyond. The murmuring river tickled at the edge of his hearing as he scanned up and down the valley, checking for movement, the glint of a weapon or the hunched shape of a rider.

He twisted round and whispered to Alexandra, "All seems to be quiet." Throwing his right leg up over Mist's neck, he slid to the ground, then turned and lifted his arms to help her off.

She took his left hand and slid off as he had—and into his arms. For a heartbeat they said nothing, their gazes locked.

Illuminated by the moonlight, her eyes glowed with some emotion he couldn't identify, her lips gleamed softly, and her skin looked so smooth and delicate it was almost translucent.

"I owe you my life," he whispered, tracing the outline of her cheek with a finger.

"Likewise," she said with a smile, raising their linked hands and touching his fingers to her lips.

The breath caught in his throat. "Next time we meet, let us have just the simple riding lesson we intended, if you agree? No Armstrongs, no Grahams?"

Her smile widened, and she held his hand to her chest, tilting her chin mischievously. "No falling off."

She has a sense of humour. Unusual for a lady. Every moment he spent with her, she entranced him a little more.

Even if she *was* English and should be out-of-bounds. But now her mouth was close—*so close*—and so inviting, he couldn't stop himself.

"But perhaps a little of this," he murmured, touching her lips with his, catching the merest hint of mint, and then continuing to brush feather-light kisses along her jawline, then to her earlobe and down her exquisite neck.

～

A t the touch of Michael's lips, every inch of Alex's skin felt alive and sparkling.

For a moment they melded together, his mouth searching for hers, the depth of their kiss stealing her breath and chasing every thought from her mind.

But after only a minute, he sighed and pushed her gently away. "I must go, before I do something I will regret. Or before someone finds us and we have to hide again." His mouth twisted into a crooked smile. "I have a feeling I outstayed my welcome with Lord Kersdale."

At this, she laughed, and it broke the spell he'd woven over her. "I could always take you back in chains, say I caught you escaping."

His mouth twisted into a crooked smile. "And I would never live it down, being caught by a lassie. Even if that lassie can out-ride every man I ever met."

A shoulder lifted. "I'm nothing special."

Tilting her chin with his fingers, he looked deep into her eyes. "I disagree. I think you are very special." Then his eyes crinkled. "Or mayhap 'tis the horse who does it. He is a fine beastie, after all."

She snorted. "You make me laugh."

"Likewise," he replied, with a glint in his eye, catching her into his arms again and planting a quick kiss on her lips.

"Now, if I can concentrate enough to direct my horse on the right paths rather than thinking of you, I'll away to Jedburgh and deliver my message to the queen." He glanced into the woods behind her. "Will you keep to the side of the path, and listen for any riders so you've time to hide if need be?"

She nodded.

"And will you be able to make it right with your father? Will he know it was you who helped me escape?"

Placing a finger on his lips, she whispered, "So many questions! Don't worry. I shall make it right with him. I am his only child and heir, and he can't be angry with me for long."

Whilst that was true, Michael's question gave Alex pause. She'd been so focussed on helping him escape, on getting him safely out of the barn, that she hadn't thought how to explain her absence—or the unconscious guard—to her father. *I will think on it later. There will be a way.*

Michael caught her hand in his, kissing the palm and raising it to his cheek, where she could feel the rasp of stubble on the planes of his jaw.

"Be careful, lassie," he breathed, and kissed her on the lips, tenderly this time, pulling her close to his strong chest and tangling a hand in her hair. "And dinna forget me," he added, kissing the tip of her nose.

"Likewise," she replied, chewing her lip to stop from laughing.

As he turned to his horse, his grin was so wide she could see his teeth gleam in the moonlight. "I may be some time in Jedburgh—I canna tell how long I'll have to wait before Her Grace will give me audience. But I dinna think it will be safe to send a messenger to ye. And your father may kill me if he sees me again," he added ruefully.

"I'll work on him," she said, moving to the front of his horse so she could see him as he mounted. "But know that every day around noon I shall be training Duke on the meadow here," she gestured at the flat grass beyond the Liddel Water, "and waiting to give you your riding lesson."

He nodded and bent down from the back of his horse to give her one more kiss. "Know that I *will* come. Even if it takes a week, or a month, or—pity forbid—a year. And know that I'll think of you every day, every hour, even every moment until we meet again."

She smiled up at him, and this time they said it together: "Likewise."

CHAPTER 10

A LEX WATCHED FROM the edge of the wood as the grey splashed through the stream and into Scotland.

With a farewell raise of his arm, Michael cantered off north-east up the valley, where after some miles he would skirt the hamlet of Castleton, pass the forbidding Hermitage Castle, seat of the Earl of Bothwell, and then travel north to Stobs Castle—his castle—a ride of around twelve miles.

From Stobs it was another twelve or thirteen miles to Jedburgh, where he was to meet the Queen of Scots, but Alex was unsure of the exact details of that journey, never having ridden as far as Jedburgh on her forays into Scotland.

She had visited Carlisle, the walled English town dominated by its stone fortress, and Berwick—similarly walled and fortified—with her father to sell horses, but never Jedburgh. Was it a fine town, she wondered? *It must be, if the queen visits.*

From the stories Alex had heard about Elizabeth their English queen, royalty seemed to prefer living in luxury in their palaces, where they would partake in courtly intrigue and aristocratic scandal. The world of kings and queens was a far cry from the simpler life of their subjects in the border lands, who spent their summers living with their sheep and cattle in roughly-built shielings in the high pastures, and winters in their peel towers or fortified houses, rearing livestock—or reiving those reared by others...

The Grahams of Kersdale were not one of the notorious reiving families like the Armstrongs or Elliots of Scotland or the English Charltons or Robsons. Her father, their leader, enjoyed breeding and selling horses, and their fortified keep at Kersdale and secret farmhouse here at Kershope, had helped them to avoid the worst ravages of rival clans.

But when the nights grew long and their cupboards grew bare, the Grahams had been known to ride and raid, as did almost every clan on both sides of the frontier. It was a way of life, almost a hobby for some, and for centuries the Border clans had known no other way to survive.

So meeting Michael had been eye-opening for Alex, making her wonder if there were other ways to live. Could she train horses for a living? Could she teach *others* to ride as she did? It was something to consider, to occupy her thoughts for the long days and nights until she might see him again. For Alex didn't see herself as someone's wife, keeping house and birthing babies and spending her days with embroidery or music. She needed an outlet for her restless energy and direction for her impetuous nature. Perhaps being a horse master would provide her with independence and a life she would enjoy?

Cloak wrapped around her shoulders, Alex stood lost in her thoughts, facing up the valley until her eyes watered and the rider she watched had become just a pinprick of shadow against the grey of the moonlit valley.

~

I f she hadn't been lost in daydreams, Alex might've heard the approaching rider sooner, and things might've been very different.

But the horse was almost upon her when she became aware of the drumbeat of its hooves. Panic sent her backwards into the nearest bush, pulling her dark cloak over the white of her face and shirt. With luck, the cover of her mantle and the almost-dark of the night would be sufficient to stop a hurrying reiver from noticing her.

For marauding reivers didn't only take livestock. They'd also been known to burn unprotected buildings, steal household goods, kidnap hostages—or rape any womenfolk that took their fancy.

With her horse under her, clan around her and half-armour, sword, dirk and bow to protect her, Alex didn't worry about such things—in fact, her enemies were more likely to worry about *her*.

But here in the woods on her own, with only her dagger to protect her and one working arm, she was vulnerable. It was a feeling she misliked. *I should've armed myself better when I went to release Michael.* In fact, she should've taken more time to think through the details of his rescue—like how she would explain his escape to her father. *I must learn not to be so impulsive.* Mayhap there was value in being methodical.

Holding her breath, Alex waited until the rider was well past, and she was sure that another did not follow before she lowered her cloak and looked after them. And then her heart stopped.

For the galloping horse silhouetted against the silvery grassland was a proud, powerful dark beast that she recognised as well as anything in this world. *Duke.*

How had someone managed to steal him?

But this was a time for action, not questions. Raising two fingers to her lips, Alex sent a piercing whistle across the valley, the signal she used to get Duke to come to her when he was out grazing.

The fleeing horse didn't falter, and Alex frowned. She was sure it was him. Taking a deep breath, she whistled again, louder this time, and for a moment the horse seemed to hesitate. But the rider applied his spurs, and Duke surged forwards again, racing towards the Armstrong stronghold at Mangerton and away from his mistress and his home.

Fury burned through Alex's body, and before she knew it she was running towards the border, cloak streaming behind her, feet flying across the rough ground.

It was only when her feet splashed into the icy-cold shallows of the river that sense overtook reaction, and she pulled to a halt, breath heaving and injured arm aching. Glancing quickly around, she cursed herself. For her impetuous nature had put her in even more danger than she had already faced in the wood. All it would take was *one* rider to find her here, alone, injured and lightly-armed, and she could be dead. *Or worse.*

For a full minute she stood there, agitation warring with caution and the desire for revenge vying with despair.

Angry tears coursed down her cheeks; she took one step towards her horse, and then one step back to the forest, her actions mirroring her uncertainty as the debate raged inside her.

Eventually, sense won out. Retribution would come better from a band of riders mounted on fast horses and chasing Duke on a hot trod, than from one lonely girl on foot and unarmed.

With one last longing look up the valley at her disappearing horse, she turned back for the wood, shoulders slumped and tears smearing her vision so that she could hardly see one foot in front of the other. *I'll get you back, Duke,* she vowed. *Somehow. I'll get you back.*

CHAPTER 11

NOT UNTIL ALEX had once more reached the relative safety of the wood did the implications of Duke's theft overtake her sorrow at losing her horse. For Duke hadn't been grazing in the enclosure with Mist and the other beasts, he'd been stabled in the barn with the rest of the Grahams' best breeding stock and their more valuable livestock. So for him to have been stolen, not only had someone discovered their secret hideout, but they'd somehow forced their way into the barn.

Or mayhap not, she thought, remembering how she had left Peter unconscious by the doorway. Could it've been just one lucky thief who had happened on their unprotected bastle house in the dark?

No. For if that'd been the case, would he not have taken one of the animals in the paddock, which were easier reached and less likely to get him discovered? And how had he got there? Why would he have left his own mount behind?

Her misgivings growing, Alex increased her pace until she was jogging along the drove road, clenching her teeth against the pain in her shoulder and arm, which had grown worse from the rough treatment she'd given it over the last hour or so.

It was the memory of the Armstrong reivers chasing them along this very track that spurred her into a full-blown sprint. What if those ruffians had left some lookouts in the wood to watch for activity after they'd lost their quarry this afternoon? Could a vigilant scout have spotted her and Michael, as they slipped around the stone in the dark, and discovered the farmhouse that way?

Yes. That must be how it happened. She was convinced now. *It is all my fault.* If she hadn't agreed to meet Michael yesterday afternoon this would never have transpired.

So what if he looked like a Norse god and seemed to care about horses more than any man she'd ever known? She'd let her feelings get in the way of prudence, and now their stronghold had been discovered and her whole clan would suffer.

If anything has happened to Father I'll never forgive myself. Heart in her mouth, she raced around the grey stone and down the secret track to discover the fate of her family.

~

The scene that met Alex back at the bastle house was worse than she imagined.

Frightened livestock huddled in the far corner of the enclosure, eyes wide and nostrils flaring. Across the paddock, a burning hay rick sent orange flames high into the sky, black smoke swirling and the acrid smell pervading the whole scene.

Losing the winter fodder to fire would be a disaster for the clan, and everyone had pitched in to help put out the blaze.

Illuminated by the fire, a chain of people passed water

buckets to throw on the flames, and Alex ran to join them, passing the sprawling bodies of two strange men as she went, arrows bristling from one and a well-placed lance from the other.

Slotting into the line beside Hob, Alex hissed at him as she held out her good hand for the next bucket. "Is my father safe?"

Hob almost dropped the bucket he was holding. "You're here! We thought you'd been kidnapped."

"I...escaped." *They thought I was kidnapped!* That might provide an excuse for her absence. Mayhap she was in luck. "And Father?"

"He tends Peter's wound."

Peter. The man she'd left unconscious in front of the barn. "Is he badly hurt?"

Hob lifted a shoulder. "Been stabbed."

Tears sprang to Alex's eyes as the next bucket passed through her hands. *'Tis my fault.* Fearing to hear the answer, she asked, "Was anyone else harmed?"

"No, but—" Hob turned to look her in the eye, his face wary. "You know they took your horse?"

Alex clenched her jaw. "Yes. I tried to follow him but he was too fast."

Hob grimaced. "Evan is off to Kersdale to raise a trod. We thought we would be seeking you also. How did you escape?"

Thinking quickly, Alex pulled the dagger from her boot. "I wasn't the docile woman they thought."

A grin split Hob's round face. "Even injured, you're fiercer than most men." He jerked his chin over his shoulder at the farmhouse. "You should go tell your father you are returned. He would be out here rounding up a posse if he didn't have Peter to doctor."

~

"Father!" Alex stepped into the main room of the bastle house.

Looking up from where he tended his patient, Simon's face visibly relaxed. "You're safe!" He motioned her over to Evan's bedside, then frowned. "How did you escape?"

In answer, she produced the dagger. "You taught me well."

Simon gave a strained smile. "'Tis easy seen you're my daughter. Was it the Armstrongs?"

"I think so."

Her father clenched his jaw. "I *knew* we shouldn't have spared that prisoner. 'Tis he who injured Peter and gave entrance to the raiders."

"But he isn't an Armstrong, father."

"How say you that? He took your horse, kidnapped you, almost killed Peter and set fire to the hay!"

This goes from bad to worse! "'Twas not he who took me. And the Scots queen wouldn't accept an Armstrong as messenger. The Scots hate them almost as much as we do. Could it not be that the Armstrongs spied him bringing me here when I was injured, waited till nightfall and then broke in, stole my horse and took *him* as hostage?"

"Did you see any of this when you were captured?" His eyes darkened. "And *how* did they endeavour to capture you, when you were asleep up here?"

Alex thought fast. "I awoke in a sweat from my injury and went outside for some cool air. But I know 'twas not the captive who kidnapped me or stole my horse, for I saw the man that rode Duke, and would've followed, had I not been on foot." Now was the time to change the subject. "Hob said my uncle is raising a trod to win Duke back?"

"'Twas to win *you* back, not the horse." A groan from his patient returned Simon's attention to the man before him, and he put fresh wadding on the wound. "I'll tell him to stand down. We can claim redress through the warden at the next truce day. 'Tis only a horse."

"He is not *just* a horse. He's *my* horse. Who I've trained like the Italian masters. And he's one of your breeding stallions."

Simon's face hardened; an expression that meant his mind was made up. "Even so, a horse isn't worth risking my men against the Armstrongs." He pointed at Peter. "They've already done enough damage."

Alex pressed her lips together, remembering her promise to Duke that she would get him back. A hot trod would have a chance, but every hour they waited it would make it harder to retrieve him. And she daren't leave him with ill-mannered men who would treat him like a beast of burden rather than a highly-trained palfrey, and might even abuse him.

But she had one last argument which would be sure to sway her father. "Mayhap. But if we leave the thief to get away, he will spread word of our location, and we'll no longer be safe here. We need to find him and silence him."

At this, her father's eyes narrowed, and he took a moment before answering, long enough that Alex thought for a second that she'd won him round. *But no.* "We'll have to abandon this place, nevertheless, since they've destroyed our winter fodder and we don't know how many others were hiding in the woods and watching." He shook his head decisively. "Our time here is over. We'll repair to Kershope come the morn."

Alex stood and turned for the door, so he wouldn't see her angry tears. "I'll gather my things and make ready, then."

But she hadn't given up on Duke. She had a plan, a simple plan that would be easy to execute. *If Father and the family won't help, I'll just have to get him myself.*

CHAPTER 12

SUNDAY 6TH OCTOBER, 1566

B Y THE TIME they arrived at Stobs, an elegant keep with a pinnacled round tower, Mist was almost on his knees, and Michael fared not much better. It had been a long, emotional day with much hard riding and plenty to occupy his mind.

Handing the horse to a yawning groom, Michael stumbled into the main tower and up the three stone flights to his chamber, waving away his housekeeper's offer of ale or cheese. "I've nae energy for eating," he said, pushing open the heavy oak door. Pausing only to pull off his mud-splattered boots, he fell onto the feather mattress of his canopied bed and fell instantly asleep.

It was hours later that Michael awoke, having forgotten in his fatigue to instruct anyone to rouse him at dawn. *The queen!* he thought, splashing his face with cold water from the bowl on his wooden dresser and running fingers through his tousled hair. *I must hasten to Jedburgh.*

But as he rushed to the door, he caught a glimpse of himself in the looking glass on the wall and stopped short. *I canna address the queen in these travel-stained garments.* Rifling quickly through his armoire, he dressed hurriedly in clothes more suitable to attend court and packed a clean shirt into a saddlebag.

Down at the stables, he discovered Mist looking much refreshed—more-so than he himself felt—after a belly-full of hay and a reviving bucket of oats. He'd intended to take one of the other horses, but Mist was his favourite and, maybe because of that, the fittest and strongest. Michael scratched the grey's nose. "A trip to Jedburgh to see the queen, lad? Could ye manage that?" Of course, he got no reply, just a level gaze from Mist's dark eyes and a velvety muzzle inspecting Michael's pockets lest any oats should somehow have ended up there. Instructing the groom to get the horse saddled and ready, Michael made for the kitchens.

Over a hasty breakfast, he quizzed his housekeeper, Mrs Beattie, on local news, and discovered that the earl of Bothwell was abroad and flexing his muscles as chief lieutenant of the Scottish Marches. It was a title recently bestowed upon the unpopular James Hepburn by Mary Stuart herself, much to the displeasure of the senior wardens, who resented having this relatively young man placed in authority over them. But some said that he was a favourite of the queen and a stalwart member of her Privy Council, and that was why he'd been appointed to this role.

Perhaps fortunately, courtly duties in Edinburgh had kept Bothwell from the last truce day at Lochmabenstone, for he was an arrogant man who would doubtless have upset the English wardens without even trying. Michael considered himself lucky to have had little to do with the ambitious earl until now. *But that luck might change when I arrive at Jedburgh and present myself to the queen.*

Wiping his hands in a napkin, Michael stood, strapped on his sword and made for the door. He had a duty to perform: a message to take to his monarch. There was no benefit in worrying about a rogue earl who, if rumours were correct, had his sights set higher than the marches of the borderlands and would have little interest in a mere deputy warden.

The hardest thing about Alex's plan had been persuading Hob to join her. And that took all of half a minute. After that it was easy.

She'd already swapped into more suitable clothes for travelling and, under the guise of packing had gathered a little food, her breastplate, helmet and weapons.

Once outside, all remained chaos, the hayrick still smouldering despite being doused by scores of water buckets. With people flying in every direction, it was easy to pull Hob aside, wait for him to gather a hank of rope and some discarded arms and then for them both to sneak a couple of horses out of the enclosure without being noticed.

Before long, they'd reached the grey stone. Hob helped her onto her borrowed horse and as the first fingers of dawn light spread across the eastern sky they galloped up the Liddesdale valley in pursuit of Duke and his captor.

Crouching over the chestnut's neck, Alex had to hope that they'd got away in time; that this trod, tiny as it was, would be enough to bring results and return her stolen horse to where he belonged. For anything else would be unthinkable.

Riding away from his castle and along the narrow wooded valley of the Slitrig Water, Michael made for higher ground. Rounding the flank of White Hill and passing between it and Peat Law, he made good time in the early part of his ride. It was a route with little to recommend it except speed, lying as it did over bleak, featureless moorland with only scrub grass and the occasional sparrow-hawk for company.

It was only when the track rolled over the top of Hoggfield Hill that the view opened out and the wide panorama of hills and glens leading eastwards towards Bonchester and on to Jedburgh gave a more pleasant aspect to his ride. After watering his horse at the well in Bonchester Bridge, Michael passed between Bonchester Hill and the mighty Rubers Law, following the Rule Water as far as Hall-rule Mill before branching over the hills once more, aiming for Langlee and thence to Jedburgh.

But all the time that Mist trotted along peaty rabbit tracks, or picked his way carefully down heather-covered hillsides, Michael's mind was in turmoil. Now that his mission to meet the queen was underway and he had time to think for himself, his thoughts returned to the events of the last few days and his meetings with Alexandra in particular.

It wasn't that he hadn't met a pretty lass before, nor held one in his arms or traded kisses. But there was something different about Alexandra—a courage and spirit that made him want to get to know her better. *Much* better.

Which was the problem.

He could not—*should* not—meet her again, despite the promises he'd made in the thrall of emotion. Because it could go nowhere, and there could be no future for them.

Michael's heart felt like someone had squeezed it dry, his shoulders sagging as if they carried a sack filled with fodder and his eyes smarting as he set his face into the brisk wind that rustled the long grass and ruffled through his hair.

For as an *English* woman, Alexandra was out-of-bounds. Scots law forbade intermarriage without a licence—with the death penalty as a deterrent.

Admittedly, many Marchmen ignored this edict, which

was why names like Hall and Graham were prevalent on both sides of the border and why Michael had initially assumed that Alexandra was Scottish.

Yes, his friendship with Alexandra might be in its early days and marriage a distant and unlikely option, but it would not be honourable to have liaisons with her that could lead nowhere. And as a deputy warden, it was Michael's duty to *uphold* the law, not break it. Was he not the one who spoke out the strongest against reivers and did his best to discourage it in his area?

But, maybe for the first time in his life, upholding his principles made Michael feel like he was in the wrong, rather than his usual assuredness of being in the right. It made his chest ache and his head feel like it were pinched in a clamp.

However he could see no way around it. She was English, and off-limits to him; any relationship between them was forbidden and would undermine his wardenship.

It was because his mind was elsewhere, and not concentrating on his travels, that things then took a turn for the worse.

Traversing some softer ground after he had rounded Watch Knowe and passed Langlee, Mist slipped and stumbled, and within a few paces he became noticeably lame. With a curse, Michael dismounted, hoping that it was merely a stone in the horse's hoof.

Running a hand down the horse's foreleg to pick up his foot, Michael felt some heat and the beginning of a swelling just above the fetlock. With a sigh, he straightened and assessed the injury. "That looks to be a sore one, boy," he said, patting Mist's neck, worry gnawing at his insides. "But if you can make it to the town you can rest there."

In this secluded glen, the Black Burn ran close to the track, its peaty waters undercutting the high banks and glistening darkly even on the brightest of days. But near to where Michael had stopped was a wider spot with a gravelly shelf, where he was able to lead Mist into the cool water, hoping to reduce the heat and swelling.

While he ministered to the horse, Michael pulled some bread and cheese from his saddlebags, since it was now well past lunchtime. Sitting on the mossy edge of the stream with his simple repast, he tried not to let himself dwell on the poor omens of this trip. He could only hope things would get better when he got to Jedburgh and met with the queen.

CHAPTER 13

I T WAS NOT far to Mangerton Tower, the main seat of the Liddesdale Armstrongs.

Hidden in the rough wood that overlooked the eastward side of the imposing tower, Alex and Hob squatted in the cover of some evergreen shrubs as their horses picked at blades of grass in the small clearing behind them.

Below them, the tower sat in a shallow valley near to the Liddel Water. It was a solid rectangular structure, which would be impenetrable without a large force or a battery of canon. If Alex had needed into the tower, her cause would already have been hopeless. However, the arrogance of the Armstrongs was evident in the outer defences. Or rather, the lack of them.

Rather than the high stone barmkin wall favoured by most Border lairds, the tower was surrounded by a mere wooden picket fence atop a shallow ditch. Admittedly the fence was near five foot high and the wooden staves were pointed at their tops, facing outward to make them harder to scale. But it wasn't the ten-foot wall they might've found, and the seed of an idea began to grow in Alex's brain.

Inside the enclosure were cooking fires, a hay store, lean-to buildings—and the object of their search. Tethered along one side of the bailey were a score of horses, and amongst them a glossy black that Alex recognised instantly. *Duke.*

With a grin of relief, Alex motioned Hob back to the clearing where they could talk more easily.

Pulling a pack of bread and cheese from her saddlebag, she hunkered on the mossy ground under an ancient oak and passed Hob a share of the food. "If we wait until nightfall, and you help me over the fence, I believe I can get Duke out of there."

His mouth full of food, Hob looked sideways at her, then nodded significantly at her sore arm.

"Yes, even injured. Duke will get me out safely."

Hob shrugged eloquently. He'd learned long ago not to argue with Alex when her mind was made up.

∼

Situated at the intersection of five different roads, the market in Jedburgh was a broad, cobbled expanse surrounded by tall buildings that crowded in as if to peer at the stallholders displaying their wares.

The offerings were many and varied—one wide-girthed merchant spread bolts of fine linen and deep-dyed wool on a two-wheeled barrow; another hook-nosed old man sold trinkets and buttons from a cloth-covered table; nearby, a farmer's wife sat wearily behind wicker baskets overflowing with vegetables; and a one-eyed man in a leather jerkin offered a brace of pigeon to anyone who would give him a silver sixpence.

Someone, somewhere, was selling hot meat pies, and the smell of the savoury gravy wafting across the marketplace made Michael's stomach rumble as he pushed past crowds of chattering townsfolk and made his way to the nearby hostelry that was his destination.

Situated a little way down the high street, the Spread Eagle had originally been one of the town's defensive towers, and its thick stone walls and the narrow windows on the lower floors attested to that. At the back of the large building, between it and a townhouse owned by Lord Home, there was stabling, and it was there that Michael entrusted Mist to the care of a wiry stable-boy. With the inducement of an extra ha'penny each time, the lad agreed to stand the leg in cold water thrice a day, which Michael hoped would reduce the swelling and hurry the healing.

As the major inn of the town, the Spread Eagle was where the queen and the most important of her entourage would reside, and staying there would make his job easier. But Michael was relieved to hear that her party hadn't yet reached the town, although they'd sent word to prepare meat, drink and lodgings for the nobles and gentlemen who'd been summoned to attend Her Grace.

The harassed-looking innkeep, with his once-white apron and floury hands made a show of reluctance at the thought of finding space for another guest, until the clink of silver shillings managed to secure Michael a small room up in the garret—one that was no doubt meant for a servant, but Michael was just glad to be in the same lodgings as the queen.

His next stop was a livery stable, not far away and next to the horse market, where he would rent a riding horse to use while Mist was lame. The proprietor—a burly man with a red face and thin hair plastered over his balding pate—led Michael over to the rank of horses he had available for hire. But, rather cannily perhaps, the route the man took went past a fine-looking bay that caught Michael's eye. "What about that one?" he asked, pointing at the gelding.

"Ah, 'e be not for hire, that 'un. Too good for that. I thought to mebbe keep 'im for mysel'." He sucked air through his teeth and looked Michael up and down. "But I could p'raps make an exception for a fine gent like yoursel'," the liveryman said, rubbing his meaty hands together. "Twenty guineas, and cheap at half the price."

Michael scratched his chin, knowing he was being baited like a fish on a line but sizing up the horse's strong back and clean limbs and liking what he saw. "Can I try him?"

With a glint in his eye, the ostler went to collect a saddle, and twenty minutes later, he'd made a sale, even if it had been negotiated down somewhat from the full price he'd hoped for.

Sitting astride the bay, Michael was reminded of how it had felt to ride Alexandra's stallion. *Spirit*, he decided to call the horse. There was a power there, just waiting to be tapped. Spirit's canter felt like he was riding on air, his trot like it could carry him forever. A horse that was worthy of Alexandra's training methods.

The thought hit Michael like a sledgehammer.

Had he not resolved never to meet with the English-woman again? So why was he thinking about training Spirit with her? A sigh escaped him as he rode the short distance back up the high street to the inn. His mind may have made the most sensible decision, but if he was to judge by the ache in his chest, it was obvious that his heart hadn't yet caught up with that arrangement.

Maybe a hearty meal and some tankards of ale were in order, to dull his feelings sufficiently that he would sleep without dreaming of raven-haired horsewomen with lustrous eyes and mischievous smiles.

~

F or once, the weather was on their side. Alex gave a silent prayer of thanks for the clouds overhead, which obscured the moon, hiding their movements in the deep shadow of the palisade. At a corner far from the tower doorway, and even further from the entrance gate, Hob helped Alex onto his shoulders, from where she could grasp a rope he'd already thrown up and looped over the top of a fence paling.

It was difficult, with only one arm working, and Alex was grateful for the stout canvas of her breeches and the protection offered by her leather breastplate, having elected for the manoeuvrability of the lighter garment rather than the more cumbersome, if more defensive, metal armour.

Of course, Hob had tried to persuade her to let *him* go and liberate Duke, since all his limbs were working properly. But she'd persuaded him that it would only work this way, as she was the better rider of the pair, and it needed her special bond with Duke to make the plan possible.

He'd grudgingly agreed but insisted that she spent the bulk of the day catching up on lost sleep while he kept guard, longbow constantly by his side and arrow nocked at the ready.

So here they were, hours later, the two of them assailing the fortified tower of the most notorious clan in the whole of the Scottish borders, relying on luck, darkness and a willing stallion to make good their escape.

Perhaps not the most foolproof plan she had ever hatched...

A teeth-clenching minute later, Alex dropped silently onto the beaten earth inside the palisade. Standing immobile for a few seconds, she held her breath, listening for the shout that would indicate she'd been spotted.

But all remained quiet; she seemed to have made her

entrance unseen. Slowly exhaling, she started her careful progress towards the tethered horses.

Five minutes, she'd agreed with Hob, and she was glad she hadn't been more optimistic. Because creeping across the bailey, in the shelter of whatever buildings she could find took longer than she might've thought, and she'd only just reached the horses when part two of their plan swung into action.

Taking a leaf from the Armstrong's own book, two flaming arrows sailed over the wooden fence in quick succession, carefully aimed by Hob at the pile of hay stored at the other side of the enclosure. The dried grass quickly caught light, and a cry of alarm sounded from somewhere nearby. While Alex crept up to Duke and quickly worked on his tie lines, footsteps hammered across the bailey and shouts of command echoed through the night as the occupants of the tower hastened to attend to the fire.

Quickly knotting one of Duke's ropes into a rough head-collar, with two reins for guidance, Alex turned the stallion to face into the courtyard and used a conveniently placed barrel to scramble on board.

It felt good to be back up there, and the solid width of him was as reassuring as the fact that he seemed unperturbed by the nearby fire—unlike the other horses, which had started to shift nervously, eyes staring and nostrils snorting.

Alex sat quietly for a minute until she judged that Hob should've made it back to the wood, and until it seemed that all the Armstrongs who were going to attend the fire had already done so, making her less likely to meet a hurrying foe.

Now! she thought, and urged Duke into a run, aiming him at the part of the palisade she'd earmarked earlier, gripping with her thighs and gathering him together, concentrating his energy into his hindquarters, ready for the huge leap ahead of them.

For that was her plan. Rather than trying to burst through the gate, risking the swords and spears of her adversaries, Duke was to tackle the wooden palisade; a jump that was formidable but, she hoped, within his capabilities.

Heart in her mouth, she leaned forward and concentrated on keeping her balance as his strong muscles bunched underneath her and then sprung over the wooden obstacle.

For a moment it felt like they were flying, and she would've laughed with glee—if it wasn't for the colossal drop they faced on the far side.

Shifting her weight so she now leaned back, but still perpendicular to the ground, Alex held tightly onto her makeshift reins with her one good hand, hoping that Duke would see well enough in this moonless night to spot the landing and make a clean getaway.

For if he stumbled, she would surely slip from his glossy back, and then she would be at the mercy of the Armstrongs. And those ruffians would no doubt be enraged by this audacious theft—as they would see it—and disinclined to mercy.

She couldn't risk that.

Clamping her legs around Duke's sides, Alex sent up a wordless prayer as his hooves touched the grass at the far side of the castle compound.

CHAPTER 14

W E MADE IT! Alex thought exultantly as Duke bounded towards the safety of the wood. *The plan worked!* All that remained was the third part of her scheme— to meet up with Hob and race home before the Armstrongs came after them.

Slowing Duke as they entered the wood, she scanned the dark shapes of the trees, looking for the tell-tale presence of Hob or the horses. But something was wrong.

The clearing where they'd waited earlier was eerily empty, and the hairs on the back of her neck started to prickle. Duke tensed underneath her too, sensing that something was amiss, and she debated whether to make a run for it.

But she didn't think quickly enough.

The shadows around the clearing suddenly took form. Not the ancient trees that'd surrounded them in the daytime, but a band of riders who stepped forward at some silent signal from their leader, hemming her in and leaving no avenue for escape.

"Halt!" the lead rider cried. "Who be you and what is your

business here?" Sitting atop a sturdy grey garron, he was a short but powerful-looking man with an arrogant expression and a carefully-trimmed beard, carrying a round shield emblazoned with the lion rampant of Scotland.

Behind the stranger she spotted Hob, bound and gagged aboard his horse, and attached by a long rope to a thickset guard in black armour. Hob's eyes were wide and his pale skin whiter than ever, but his shoulders remained defiant.

Alex took some courage from her friend, and jutted her jaw. "Alexandra Graham of Kersdale, retrieving my horse," she pointed down at Duke, "who was stolen by the Armstrongs of Mangerton last night. And who be you to accost a lady so?"

"James, Earl of Bothwell and Chief Warden of the Queen's Marches, here by Her Grace's orders to deal with trouble-makers." He looked theatrically around him. "I see no sign of a burning turf. Why do you carry out an illegal trod?"

"'Tis not illegal," Alex protested. "They stole my horse. I *saw* them take him last night, but was unable to give chase at the time."

"So you say. But this should've been taken to your warden, not into your own hands."

She narrowed her eyes. "And if we'd waited for the warden, I wouldn't be sitting here, atop my own horse, twenty-four hours later."

"No matter. We'll determine the rightness of this later." Bothwell motioned three men forwards. "Tie her up and take her and the lad to Hermitage while the rest of us attend to these Armstrongs." Wheeling his horse around, he added, almost to himself, "The lass may have done us a service, causing a distraction with the fire."

~

Alex had *heard* of Hermitage Castle—everyone in this part of the Borders had heard of the notorious keep. But she'd never been this close and would never have chosen to be.

As they trotted along the entrance track, the tall stone walls of the castle loomed ahead of them through the darkness like a menacing giant. Alex tried not to be intimidated, but this supreme example of a defensive structure was brutal, yet impressive in a somewhat grim way.

Surrounded by bleak and open moorland, its location alone was daunting. With a long approach to its site high in the valley of the Hermitage Water, defenders behind their narrow arrow-slits would have ample opportunity to pick off any attackers before they got close. And then when you *did* get close, thick sandstone walls soared overhead, their grey solidity and imposing squareness giving the message that this dark edifice was built purely for defence—against the English, most likely, Alex thought with the ghost of a wry smile—rather than for the comfort of its inhabitants.

Once within hailing distance, a loud voice emanating from beside a glowing brazier on the castle ramparts challenged them to identify themselves and their business.

The guard leading Alex hollered back, "Prisoners from the earl," and they were allowed to continue unchallenged.

Traversing the narrow track alongside the long west wall, Alex's skin crawled at the thought of what might come next. Hermitage's prison tower was infamous as the spot where a previous laird, Sir William Douglas, had left a rival to starve to death. It was said to be a grim pit, devoid of light, air and sanitation, and Alex gritted her teeth, steeling herself to face this ordeal.

Rounding the large south-west tower, they approached the central part of the castle. Its entrance seemed tiny, flanked as it was on three sides by four stories of forbidding stone. With every step they took, Alex felt smaller and more insignificant, which she was sure was one of the main purposes of the ominous structure.

And then they were inside, passing under not one but *two* portcullises into a central cobbled courtyard where they dismounted.

Here, at last, there was a slight improvement to their situation. "Take the lady to the first-floor prison," the guard said, throwing Alex's rope to one of his subordinates.

So not the foul dungeon, then. Alex stood her ground, squaring her jaw at the tall soldier. "And my brother too."

He squinted down his nose at her, then jerked his chin at the other man. "Aye. Leave more room down below for the Armstrongs, when the earl returns."

Alex glanced sideways at Hob, who looked as worried as she. "Be thankful we won't have the Armstrongs as bedfellows," she whispered as they were led up the narrow turnpike stair.

But that was the best that could be said about their new lodgings. For the small room they were thrown into was dank and bare, with only a pile of dirty rushes in one corner to make some semblance of a bed, and a bucket in another corner for hygiene. *Duke's stable is probably more comfortable*, Alex thought miserably as she and Hob huddled against the far wall.

"We can only hope the earl doesn't tarry long with the Armstrongs," she said, trying to lift Hob's spirits, "and then we may be out of here." For in a place like this, escape by any other means seemed unlikely, if not impossible.

CHAPTER 15

ALEX STRAIGHTENED HER spine and tried not to tremble. But the earl of Bothwell was notorious in these parts, and here she was, barefoot before him on the cold stone floor, hands tied tightly behind her back, dirty and tired after a sleepless night in his dank cells.

In contrast, the earl looked hearty and well-rested, sitting at his large hewn-oak table and breaking his fast with a bowl of oat porridge and some unidentifiable beverage in a pewter flagon. "What have you to say for yourself?" he asked, gesticulating with his spoon.

With a tilt of her chin, Alex looked him in the eye. "I say that you have imprisoned us unlawfully, and when Forster hears of it, there will be repercussions."

"Repercussions, you say?" Bothwell's eyebrows arched sceptically.

"Yes. We were carrying out a legal trod, and you had no right to imprison us." She hardened her expression, glad that he couldn't see the butterflies in her stomach. "But if you return our horses and give us safe passage to Kersdale, I will speak with my father, and plead with him not to let the warden carry out any reprisals."

Bothwell nodded slowly, looking at her appraisingly, and for a moment she thought she might have won their freedom. But then he stood, carefully wiped his mouth on a napkin, and walked around the table until he stood before her.

At the fruity smell of alcohol on his breath, and the evil glitter in his eye, she almost took a step backwards. But she set her jaw and tried not to flinch as he put a finger on her bottom lip, then ran it slowly down her chin.

Unlike when Michael had touched her, when every inch of her skin had come alive, at the earl's touch she felt nothing but revulsion.

"Fiery little thing, aren't you?" he said with a sneer, as his finger continued southwards, and flicked open the ties of her chemise.

At this, Alex had to laugh. "Little, you say?" She pulled herself to her full height, made sure that her contempt for him showed on her face, and looked him in the eye—for he was no taller than she.

A pulse throbbed in his temple, and his eyes narrowed. Drawing back a hand, he made as if to strike her.

Alex turned her cheek, heart hammering as she waited for the impact of his blow, and then gasped when a tall, neatly-dressed woman with mousy-blonde hair entered the great hall.

The newcomer's head jerked up in anger at the sight that met her eyes. "James!"

Her sharp voice stayed Bothwell's hand, and he spun on his heel. Immediately contrite, he opened his arms. "Jean, my darling! How did you sleep?"

She ignored his question, and snapped a finger in Alex's direction. "What goes on here?"

The earl affected innocence. "I was merely questioning the prisoner," he ran a hand down the sleeve of his doublet and pinched at an imaginary speck of dust, "in the hope of eliciting some clues to help with today's raid." Turning his back on Alex, he returned to his breakfast and sat down. "But the wench knows nothing," he added dismissively.

His wife's eyebrows raised sceptically. "If she knows nothing, then why is she still here? Guard!" She motioned to the beefy man who stood silently at the main entrance to the hall. "Escort the prisoner back to the dungeons."

Alex let out a long breath, tension seeping from her limbs as the guard spun her around and prodded her towards the central part of the castle.

Ridiculing the earl might have provoked a beating, but it had saved her—this time—from being molested. For Bothwell's reputation as a brute and a womaniser was well-known, even over the border in England, and he was already on his second marriage.

Stumbling down the stone stairs as the guard jabbed at her with the butt of his lance, Alex chewed her lip. She had been lucky, this time, that Bothwell's wife had intervened. But if the earl took it into his head to 'question' her again, she knew the outcome might not be quite so benign, and the thought of that chilled her to the core.

Bothwell hunkered in the bracken fringing the Billhope Burn, doglock rifle cocked and held tightly against his shoulder, eyes fixed on the turn in the track ahead where his quarry would appear.

It was a dank morning, drops of dew fringing the long grass, mist rising ponderously from the low-lying ground, and clouds bathing the hilltops, so that visibility was limited to a few hundred yards.

But he could see well enough for this hunt. The deer that roamed Stob Fell and Tudhope Hill were known to drink at the shallow pool just below his position. And one of his men had reported a particularly impressive stag, one whose head would adorn the wall of Bothwell's great hall at Hermitage, and whose meat would fill his belly for days to come.

His mouth watered at the thought of trenchers of dark venison, running with gravy and filling his nostrils with their rich, gamey aroma. He could almost taste it, and his stomach grumbled in anticipation.

Gritting his teeth, Bothwell turned his mind from thoughts of food. On a still, heavy day like this, a small sound like that would be enough to alert his prey, and he and his small band of men—hidden on the far side of the pool in case the deer took another route—would return empty-handed.

But even in that event, he need not be dispirited. For with Whithaugh, Mangerton and Shaws cleared, and his dungeons near-full of the worst of the Armstrongs, Elliots, and sundry other supporters, Bothwell's Liddesdale campaign could be deemed a success. And sufficiently productive that he could justify a few hours this morning to fill his larder.

A grim smile played on his lips. This was the best kind of day. The kind of day he lived for. A morning spent hunting deer, an afternoon giving the Armstrongs of Gilnockie his attentions, and then a ride for Cowdenknowes on the morrow to meet the queen en-route to Jedburgh.

He could almost see the queen's smile and the admiration in her eyes when she heard the news. It should raise his status and improve her opinion of him. It might even be worth another earldom.

What he *really* wanted was for her to see through the machinations of James Stewart, and give *him*, James

Hepburn, the earldom of Moray. But her half-brother, Moray, was not at fault here in the Borders, so his ambitions would likely have to wait for another day. Sadly.

The dull thud of hooves on peaty soil broke his reverie and put his senses on alert. Training his gun on the track ahead, he stilled his breathing and readied his finger on the trigger.

But the beast that came around the corner was not the stag he expected. Instead, it was the lanky figure of the ironically-named 'Little' Jock Elliot of Park, astride a sturdy brown hobbler, with a stag—*Bothwell's* stag—hanging over its rump, two arrows bristling from its neck.

Anger flared in Bothwell's chest, and with hardly a thought to the consequences, he fired at the reiver, his aim true, if a little low.

The impact of the shot, somewhere around his hip, threw Elliot from the saddle, and his horse shied and then raced off down the hill with the deer bumping on its back.

My men will catch the garron, Bothwell thought with satisfaction, *and we will yet have venison for dinner, and one less Elliot to worry about.*

Striding over to the body, Bothwell felt a glow of satisfaction at the dark smear of blood seeping from somewhere above Jock's thigh. *Got him good.* He nudged the body with the toe of his boot, leaning over to inspect his handiwork.

But like a re-animated corpse, Jock somehow produced a dagger, reared up, and lunged wildly at his attacker.

The pain Bothwell felt when the dagger sliced just above his eye was hugely out-of-proportion to the severity of the wound. But the next—to his chest, but fortunately diverted from his heart by his leather baldrick—was more life-threatening. As Elliot thrust the knife for a third time, all Bothwell could think was to use the last of his strength and grab at the blade and wrest it from the reiver.

His lacerated palm poured blood, and with the bleeding wound on his forehead almost blinding him, Bothwell swapped the dagger to his uninjured hand and swung weakly at the last place he'd seen his opponent.

But the weapon met fresh air, and, with a moan, Bothwell sank to the ground, seeking rest for his weary body and release from the pain that harangued his senses.

His brain swimming, he could only imagine that the disarmed Elliot must have seen his disadvantage and made his escape. With luck, the blackguard would be apprehended by Bothwell's men further down the glen.

But the Earl's luck was running out. His energy ebbed as his life-blood flowed richly red over the sandy banks and into the peaty waters of the Billhope Burn.

Mossy turf cushioned his cheek and the burbling of the stream faded as his vision greyed and he passed slowly into unconsciousness.

CHAPTER 16

L OUD SHOUTING ABOVE his head and jostling of the litter carrying him roused Bothwell from his swoon.

Opening groggy eyes, he blinked against the rough linen bandage drooping towards his eyelids. His chest and hand had also been bound, with expediency rather than skill, and he lay on the rough travois they'd intended for the stag. With a weak smile, he realised that the man beside him led Elliot's brown horse with the deer still tied behind its saddle.

At least our hunt was successful.

But then the shouts of his guards began to penetrate his wooly brain. It appeared there was some altercation over their entrance to Hermitage; that somehow the dungeon guards had been overcome and their prisoners had taken over the castle. Or at least most of it, for somehow Bothwell's wife had rallied the servants, and they'd barricaded themselves in the Douglas Tower, with archers on the ramparts aiming down at the portcullis and making escape for the reivers a dangerous affair.

One of the men carrying the litter noticed that Bothwell

had roused. "Sire, the Armstrongs hold the portcullis and wilna let us in. They want to parley terms."

Bothwell gave a tiny nod, then winced at the pain behind his eyes. "Tell them…send a man."

"Aye, sir."

Bothwell must've drifted off again, for the next thing he knew, someone shook his shoulder and the spike of pain roused him awake.

"Robert Elliot of Shaws is here to speak with ye, sire." This time it was the Earl's captain who spoke.

"Yes," Bothwell said shortly, remembering not to nod.

A dark figure loomed over him. "If ye want into yer castle, ye must let us free," said Elliot, his face grimy and evidence of alcohol on his breath.

They've been at my cellars. Anger flared and then fizzled as quickly as it had grown, for Bothwell had no energy for ire. "Yes," he said weakly, "Go free."

"And a pardon for all. Charges to be dropped," added Elliot.

But a fresh wave of pain wracked the earl's body, and he squeezed his eyes shut, clamping his jaw against the agony in his chest.

Distantly, he heard his captain's agreement to the reiver's terms, and then he knew no more.

~

A lex was wrong in her assumption that escape from Hermitage was impossible. It just proved impossible for her and Hob.

On the second day of their incarceration, from snippets of conversation overheard from their guards, and from the loud shouts and howls they heard emanating from the dungeons below, they surmised that the Armstrongs of

Mangerton, interred in the lower prison with some Elliots that'd also been taken by Bothwell on his night-time foray, had overcome their guards and taken over the castle—or at least parts of it.

Fortunately for Alex, the Armstrongs seemed unaware of the first-floor prison—or perhaps they were too busy looting the wine cellars to come searching for undefended women, and she and Hob were thankfully left alone.

Alone—without food or water. It was a situation which left Alex and Hob in dire straits, and it almost had her wishing for a visit from the vile earl again. For at least that way, they might have their thirst quenched and their bellies filled.

As day gave way to night, they huddled together for warmth, trying to ignore their grumbling stomachs and parched throats, wondering what the next day would bring.

CHAPTER 17

TUESDAY 8TH OCTOBER, 1566

I T TOOK UNTIL the following day, after a worrying twenty-four hours unattended by any guard and their thirst growing by the minute, for Alex and Hob's situation became clearer.

A younger, chattier guard came to service them, telling an almost unbelievable story that the earl, gravely wounded in a fight with Jock Elliot of Park, had been denied entry to the castle by the Armstrong ruffians. It was only after negotiation with one of their fellow-prisoners, Robert Elliot, that Bothwell was allowed entry in return for freedom and amnesty for all the prisoners.

Unfortunately, that amnesty did not to extend to Alex and Hob. They remained locked in their tower cell for a further week, while the earl lay feverish on his bed, seriously ill from his injuries and in danger of his life.

During that time, Alex's thoughts were dark. *What will happen to us if the earl dies? Will his successor give us a hearing? Or will the guards do away with us before then to save inconvenience?*

All they could do was to pray for a good outcome or hope

that her father might somehow hear of their plight and intervene. He might be furious at their exploits and disown her or marry her to some gouty old baron. But his wrath would be easier to face than a hangman's noose...

～

M ary stared at the hastily-scrawled note in her hand, conflicting emotions causing her shoulders to sag with relief whilst her jaw clenched in annoyance.

Here she was, at Cowdenknowes near Melrose, where she'd agreed to meet with her nobles and bishops before continuing on to Jedburgh for her justice eyres, and only *now* did her husband, Henry Stewart, Lord Darnley, send her a message to say he would not be accompanying her. *No doubt the hunting and hawking is too good over at Lennox.*

Mary scowled. If she, the queen of Scots, took her duties as lightly as the king did, the country would be in even more disarray than it already was.

And he wonders why I will not give him the crown matrimonial? Before their marriage, Darnley had bewitched her with his boyish charm and good looks. But she had quickly become disillusioned with her young husband, whose lewd behaviour had got a lady of the court with child. His immoral appetites also had him appearing drunk and debauched at various taverns around town, more often than was seemly, and frequenting male brothels on a regular basis.

He was an embarrassment who, now that he had provided her with a son and heir, would prove less trouble *away* from court than at her side. But it irked her that he would ignore her summons without good cause. For if he wished the equal power that the crown matrimonial would give him—and to succeed her if she died first—he should show more interest in affairs of parliament and more wisdom in the way he conducted himself.

Taking a deep breath, Mary tried to clear her mind and steady her emotions, so she could face her retinue with grace and composure.

But it was no good. Her stomach churned and her nerves jangled every time she thought of Darnley. *Mayhap 'twould have been better if we had never married.* Even if it meant that her young son, James, would not have been born.

For the king's arrogance and disdain for political affairs had also given the Protestant lords more cause to plot against her, egged on by the fundamentalist preacher, John Knox, whose hatred of women and Catholics was legendary. So, as a Catholic queen, in a country that had espoused Protestantism some years before, her rule was on a knife-edge.

With sufficient gold in her coffers, she could have funded an army of mercenaries and brought her fractious lords to heel by force. But in converting to Protestantism, they had cannily appropriated for themselves the vast land-holdings and tenancies of the monasteries and churches of the old faith, giving them wealth and power far above their station.

It left the royal family fighting for scraps and taxes, to the extent that Mary's father, James V, used to regularly visit his rich lords, arriving with his whole court to extract the levies he was due *in kind*, during a long stay, when he struggled to get them paid in gold.

Mary might have copied her father, if she had trusted her nobles not to poison or assassinate her while she was partaking of their hospitality. For they had already killed her beloved Italian secretary, David Riccio, and might have killed Mary herself, if it were not for the last-minute intervention of Darnley—a turnaround she still did not understand, since he had aided the plotters and led them to her chamber in the first place.

Instead, she had a few lords—mostly Catholics—who were true to her cause, and she surrounded herself with those whenever she could—like now. Huntly, Seton, Atholl, Livingston and Fleming would all accompany her to Jedburgh. And, of course, Bothwell, who would meet her there with a pack of miscreants for the assizes.

If only the king were more like Bothwell, she thought sadly. The earl might not have the height and dashing good looks of her husband, but he had tenacity, loyalty and decisiveness to offer. Not to mention at least two impregnable castles and an army of three hundred mosstroopers. *I should have waited and found me a stronger husband, one who would give me victory against the Protestant lords.*

But to Mary, her marriage vows were sacred and, unlike her much-married great-uncle, Henry VIII of England, whose rampant libido had brought about the Protestant reformation that was causing her such trouble, she could not divorce her husband just because he was inconvenient.

She squared her shoulders. *I shall just have to be strong and rule for the two of us.* Knox might think women the weaker sex, but Mary knew that he was wrong. *I will prove it.*

CHAPTER 18

WEDNESDAY 9TH OCTOBER, 1566

MICHAEL WAITED THREE days before the queen and her party arrived in Jedburgh.

He spent the intervening time attending to Mist, hunting through every bookshop and stall in the town for books on equestrianism, and getting to know his new horse. He rode Spirit twice a day, through the town and up past the ruined castle towards Lanton Hill; along the banks of the Jed Water as far as Walkersknowe; or upstream passing Ferniehirst, Sir Thomas Kerr's castle. But he didn't dare stray too far from the town for fear of missing the arrival of Mary and the chance to deliver his message.

He was back at the Spread Eagle, ministering to Mist and checking the horse's sore leg, when the sound of cheering and a great clattering of hooves on the cobbles of the High Street alerted him to the approach of the queen and her court.

Running a hand through his hair and pulling his doublet straight, Michael ran through the close to the front of the inn, ready to greet his monarch.

It was the first time Michael had seen Mary, and he had a

difficult job not to stare at her open-mouthed. Everything he'd heard about her was true—she was tall and graceful, with perfect white skin and laughing eyes. Dressed simply for travelling, she was still fashionable and comely, wearing a gold-embroidered velvet cloak over her heavy dress and white ruff, with her lustrous auburn hair looped up under a matching pearl-studded velvet hat, topped with a dancing white feather.

Sweeping a low bow as she passed, Michael knew he would be un-noticed, in the crowds and uproar that attended the queen's arrival, but felt safe in the knowledge that he'd left a message at the inn requesting an audience at her earliest convenience.

However, he was not unobserved. Rising from his bow, his eye was caught by one of the queen's ladies-in-waiting. One of her eyebrows rose by the tiniest amount, her lips curling and her cheeks dimpling. With sparkling blue eyes, waves of dark hair peeking from under her embroidered cap, and an obviously curvaceous figure hidden under her riding clothes, she was beautiful. Possibly even more so than the queen.

Amused at himself for that treasonous thought, Michael smiled back at the lady and inclined his head, wondering if this noblewoman might suffice to occupy his mind and stop him thinking about Alexandra.

For, try as he might to force reason rather than emotion to rule his actions, the Englishwoman kept invading his dreams—and daydreams. Hard riding and hard drinking over the last days in Jedburgh had done nothing to dispel the image of her teasing eyes and lithe body that danced in front of him at every opportunity. Mayhap a well-educated and flirtatious lady from Mary's court would do a better job at clearing his mind and captivating his senses...

~

Quickly installed in the best rooms at the inn, Mary immediately got down to business. A messenger arrived for Michael, accepting his petition for an audience and requesting that he attend her immediately.

His pulse racing at the thought of meeting his queen for the first time, Michael's mouth was so dry when he was ushered into her presence that he wondered if he would be able to speak his message without croaking like a frog.

The place where Mary was holding her meetings was on the first floor of the inn. Normally used for banqueting, it was a spacious room overlooking the high street which allowed a glimpse of the clock tower at the top of the Canongate. With an oak floor, thick tapestries hanging on the stone walls, and a warm fire in the hearth, it provided good protection against October chills. And with two stout guards either side of the door, good protection against any ne'er-do-wells with traitorous intentions.

Rising from his bow, Michael was met by the clear green eyes of his sovereign. No longer dressed for travelling, the queen wore her customary black as a mark of respect for her late husband, young Francis II of France. But she was no dowdy widow. Instead—resplendent in satin, taffeta and velvet; bedecked in gold enamelled jewellery; with her hair arranged in fetching curls under a lace cap and a stiff white ruff to enhance the paleness of her face—she was breathtaking.

Even in his best doublet and clean shirt, Michael still felt dull and drab in her presence, and every word he had meant to say fled from his mind. Fortunately, protocol meant that he need not speak until addressed by the queen, and he had a moment to collect his thoughts.

"Sire," she said, with an inviting tilt of her head, "I am told you 'ave a message for me from my wardens?"

"Yes, Your Grace," Michael replied, swallowing hard. "Michael Cranstoun of Stobs, Deputy Warden of the Middle March, and Laird of Penchrise, at your service." He gave another small bow.

"Come closer so I may 'ear you more easily." After five years in Scotland, Mary's voice with its clipped vowels and lilting tone held just a hint of her French upbringing.

Taking a step closer, Michael cleared his throat. "As ye may know, ma'am, we Scots wardens meet regularly wi' the English wardens to dispense justice."

The queen nodded and waved a hand at him to continue.

"When we met on Friday, the English wardens were extremely concerned about clan Armstrong. They're said to have an army of three thousand men and are the most feared reivers in the whole of the Marches. We wardens worry that if the Armstrongs invade England, there will be—" Michael paused, and for the first time since he'd entered the room, cast his eye around the other occupants. Seated on stools on either side of the queen like jewels on a crown, were her ladies-in-waiting, and one dark-haired beauty in particular...

"—reprisals," he continued with a lift of his eyebrows. "Lord Scrope, in particular, made me uneasy, as he talked about asking Queen Elizabeth to send reinforcements to Carlisle Castle." Standing taller and taking a deep breath, he caught the lovely brunette giving him an appraising look from under her lashes. "We—the Scottish wardens, that is— wondered if it might be politic to quash these troublemakers before they pitch us into a war wi' the English?"

"Aha!" Mary smiled and clapped her hands. "It is already taken care of! We 'eard word of their exploits some days ago, while still in Edinburgh, and I sent my Lord Bothwell with three-hundred 'orse to deal with them."

A great weight lifted from Michael's shoulders, and the tightness in his chest eased. But he also felt foolish.

His errand, and all his hurry, had been in vain. He could have stayed at Stobs and saved poor Mist his injury, or waited in Liddesdale with Alexandra... He nipped that thought in the bud. "My apologies for wasting your time, ma'am. But I thank ye for receiving me at such short notice." He gave another bow, and would've turned for the door, but could not leave until the queen dismissed him.

However, some of his disappointment must have shown on his face, for the beguiling lady-in-waiting leaned in to the queen and whispered in her ear.

Inclining her head, Mary addressed him again, as a little terrier nosed its way from behind her skirts and scrambled onto her lap. "It 'as been a pleasure to meet you, sire, but the occasion 'as been too short." She petted the small dog absentmindedly. "Would you do us the 'onour of joining us for dinner this evening, when we will 'ave more time for conversation? I 'ave to formally open the assizes this afternoon, but would learn more about your wardenship and your castle."

Michael had to work hard to stop himself from looking like a stranded fish as he gaped at the queen, heart hammering. Swallowing hard, he gathered his wits together. "I would be honoured, Your Grace. My humble thanks to ye."

Mary gave a small nod. "Until then."

His duty done, Michael left the chamber walking on air. Who would have thought that he, Michael Cranstoun, would dine with the queen? It was a great day for his clan and, if the pride swelling in his chest was any indication, a great day for *him* as well.

CHAPTER 19

A S IT TURNED out, Michael had very little opportunity to talk with the queen over dinner, for he was placed at a table with Sir Thomas Kerr of nearby Ferniehirst, nephew of Michael's warden, Walter Ker, and the queen's senior ladies-in-waiting. Those, he discovered, were all four of them called Mary, collectively known as 'The Maries', thanks to their childhood upbringing in the French court. They were: Mary Beaton, Mary Seton, Mary Livingston and the temptress with the dimpled smile who had caught his eye that afternoon—Mary Fleming.

To distinguish them from the queen, who it seemed was only ever called Mary—*the* Mary—he discovered that they all had nicknames.

The chauvinistic churchman John Knox had made mistaken assumptions and called Livingston 'Lusty'— Michael raised his eyebrows at that—but the girls called her 'Livvy'; Beaton was called 'Beth', her surname deriving from Béthune in Flanders; Seton, who had vowed to eternal chastity, went by 'Ebba' after the Scots' Saint Ebba, who cut off her breasts to keep men away from her—Michael's eyebrows again went skywards; and finally, Fleming was 'La Flamina', so-called, he was told, because of her flamboyant personality.

Already at ease in their company, Michael laughed at those last words from the pretty Beth Beaton and was treated to a mock bow by the mischievous Flamina, who had seated him beside her.

"But you, sire, must call me 'Flam', as my friends do." She placed her hand on his arm.

"Only if you will call me Michael," he agreed, heavily aware of her touch.

"Of course! And after dinner, we must dance," she announced, turning back to the group. "If we can find musicians." Her forehead crinkled. "Do you dance, sire?"

"After a fashion," he said with a shrug. He gestured at the packed banqueting hall; every table surrounded by members of the queen's retinue and overflowing with the food and wine the innkeep and his staff had provided; tureens of thick broth, bowls of spiced trout and platters of steaming venison. "But there wilna be much room for festivities. Mayhap something more sedentary?"

Flam gave him a sideways look. "Or we could take a turn outside. You could show us something of your town?"

"Oh, it's not *my* town," Michael took a sip of Bordeaux. "Sir Thomas would be a better guide—my castle is some miles hence." He jerked his chin westwards. "Nearer to Hawick than Jed. But I'd be happy to accompany ye."

The way he pronounced Hawick provoked some laughter from the ladies. "Hoik!" exclaimed Livingston. "How quaint!"

Michael lifted a shoulder. "'Tis the way they call it hereabouts. Galashiels gets 'Gala', and Kelso becomes 'Kelsie'. 'Tis merely our manner of speaking here in the Borders."

"Well, I, for one, would like to learn more of these Borders," said Beth.

"Yes," agreed Flam. "Let us start with Jed after dinner. If Sir Thomas is game?"

Thomas, who was as dark and wiry as Michael was fair and broad, opened his hands. "Of course, my lady."

With a flash of her blue eyes, Flam touched Michael's arm again. "And then perhaps Michael can show us his castle? During the time when the queen is busy with her council? Beth and Livvy have left their husbands at home to join the queen on this trip, so we want to have some amusement in this new place!"

Michael swallowed. What had started out as a simple dinner invitation was now turning into something more lengthy, with proposals for after-dinner perambulations and now a trip to Stobs. He had thought to return next day, but... "I would be glad to," he replied gallantly. "'Tis a pleasant ride which is easily done in a few hours."

"Well, that's settled, then!" La Flamina clapped her hands and looked round at her friends as the servants delivered sweetmeats and spiced apples to their table. "Shall we do that on the morrow?"

❧

There was little moon that night, but the air was crisp and clear, with stars pricking through the firmament and only the faintest wisps of cloud to be seen over towards the west.

As they left the Spread Eagle, Flam hooked her arm through Michael's. The ladies had dressed in simple dark cloaks, to hide their finery, and had been joined by a fifth—who, when Michael caught sight of the little terrier scampering along behind her, he realised was the queen! "Mary joins us?" he whispered to Flam.

Flam lifted a shoulder. "She loves to explore. And to dress

as a commoner." And, indeed, the queen had left her jewels and satins behind, dressing like the others in dark colours and simple fabrics.

Sir Thomas directed them to the right, up towards the marketplace. And then he, too, noticed the queen, and stopped in his tracks. "Your Grace! If you are to join us we should take some of your guard."

"Nonsense," Mary said, taking Thomas's arm. "We 'ave you and Cranstoun to protect us, fierce Borders men both, and well-armed." She looked pointedly at the knight's longsword, hanging menacingly at his side. "No-one would dare harm us."

Clenching his jaw, Sir Thomas gave a curt not. "As you wish." He caught Michael's eye, then added. "You know I would give my life for you, ma'am."

"As would I, Your Grace," Michael agreed, picking up on Ferniehirst's apprehension and hoping it would not come to that. Few locals would be foolish enough to take on a knight, let alone two well-armed and fit young men. But there was always the possibility of a plot or assassins sent from England. He squared his shoulders and resolved to be on his guard.

"So, 'tis settled." Mary's smile was charming. "Henceforth you shall be known as our protectors."

"You are too kind," Thomas replied with a small bow. "Now," he straightened and pointed to the town square. "From the marketplace, I thought we could walk up to the old castle."

The view from castle hill was spectacular, even in the dark. Standing on the grassy mound, under the ruined walls, the wide panorama of rolling hills before them was dissected by the dark, wooded valley of the Jed Water.

His voice low, Sir Thomas indicated the crumbling ramparts behind them. "The castle was occupied by the English so often that, around a hundred and fifty years ago, Balvenie ordered it demolished so they could no longer have a stronghold in our town."

As they stood taking in the night air and enjoying the view, Flam whispered to Michael, "Can we see your lands from here?"

"No," he replied in a low voice. "We face north-east. Stobs lies to the west. And there are too many hills in the way."

She nodded. "And," she looked at her hands, "will we meet Lady Cranstoun when we visit your castle tomorrow?"

Michael's eyebrows raised, unseen by Flam. Was she fishing for information? "No. There is no Lady Cranstoun. And I am laird, no' a lord."

"My apologies. You have never married?"

Michael shook his head.

"That is...surprising." She turned her face to look up at him. "You have your own castle, you're the warden. Surely you could have your pick of marriageable daughters..."

"Deputy warden," Michael corrected her, partly to give himself time to frame his reply. "I have lands but no title." He shrugged. "Father's title wasnae hereditable, and King James never corrected that in his lifetime. I am less of a prospect than you've so kindly implied."

"Ah. So you must find a titled lady. And marry for love?" She gave him a coy look.

Does she flirt with me? "That...is an option, aye."

Michael broke off. Coming up the Castlegait towards them was a dark figure, breathing heavily. Michael placed a hand on the hilt of his sword and stepped between the approaching man and the queen, pushing Flam behind him.

On the other side of the queen, Ferniehirst too had jumped to attention.

"Who goes there?" Michael demanded, and the newcomer stopped.

"'Tis only I, Livingston," came the reply.

"Brother!" Mary Livingston pushed forward and went to greet him.

"I heard you were taking the night air and wished to join you," Livingston said with a small bow. A wide man, with curly dark hair and a strong jaw, Michael was relieved to see that Livingston wore a sword. So now there were three to defend the queen, should it be necessary.

Better odds, Michael thought, catching Sir Thomas's eye and glancing significantly at the weapon.

"Welcome, Lord Livingston," said the queen, then put her hand on Thomas's arm. "Now, shall we continue with our exploration?"

From the castle they descended to the abbey, the ladies exclaiming with wonder at its size and glorious architecture.

"The English destroyed the abbey not that long ago, when Your Grace was a child, but we still use a part of it as our parish church," Sir Thomas was explaining, when the sounds of shouting and a hullabaloo came on the night air from the direction of the high street.

Spinning on his heel, Michael's jaw dropped. For a glow lit the dark sky, and it seemed to come from the direction of their lodgings. "Make haste," he shouted to their party, "It looks like a fire!"

CHAPTER 20

WHAT TROUBLE HAVE *my enemies caused now?*
Mary's skin chilled at the sight of the menacing flames, and she bent to pick up Jupiter.

In the market square, two brawny men manned the town's water pump, passing buckets of water down a hastily-formed chain of willing hands who appeared to have exited from a nearby alehouse. Their efforts were being directed by the town's red-faced blacksmith.

Stopping a safe distance from the Eagle, Mary and her group stood, open-mouthed, gazing at the nightmarish scene before them.

Mary wrung her hands. She would never forgive herself if any of the townsfolk here in this royal burgh got hurt or killed because of her rebellious lords, for they were surely responsible for starting the fire.

But maybe Flam's interest in young Cranstoun had been fortuitous, as it had taken Mary and her friends away from the inn at the time the fire was being set. If it had been an assassination attempt, it had failed...

Standing on the cobbles outside the burning building, the innkeep wrung his hands in his ash-greyed apron, his face smeared with soot and tears.

Nearby, Lord Seton, Master of Mary's household, was directing operations. A small man with a cleft chin, long nose and sandy hair, he was sending servants into the smoke to retrieve the trunks and boxes that had come with the queen's party, then directing them to stack the belongings in the centre of the street.

Ebba Seton tapped him on the shoulder. "Brother," she said, and the man turned, his face pinched with worry. Ebba gestured over her shoulder. "We have our mistress here."

Mary inclined her head.

George Seton pursed his lips in relief. "We need to find somewhere safe for Her Grace to stay until we see how things transpire here." He gestured at the smoke-filled inn.

Sir Thomas stepped forward. "I have a house just down the street that the queen can use. Down there," he pointed.

"But the queen's things and her jewels are still in there!" cried Mary Livingston. "We can't leave without them!"

Mary stared at the fire for a moment, her mind racing. Without her jewels to sell, her financial situation would be even more precarious. But what did the bible say? *Lay not up for yourselves treasures upon Earth?* And as Scotland's rightful ruler, surely God would provide?

Standing tall, she shook her head. "Jewellery can be replaced." She lifted her chin. "But I am sure Lord Seton has all in-hand. Let us go with Sir Thomas."

❧

The fire appeared to have started at the back of the building, in the kitchens, and Michael's first thought was to duck through the pend to the stables behind, to rescue Mist and Spirit. But before he could beg the queen's permission to leave their group, he sighed with relief to see the stable-boy leading his snorting horses into the street.

"Bless you," he said to the boy, slipping him a penny. Now he just needed somewhere safe to lead the scared beasts.

While Michael had been worrying about his horses, Ferniehirst had offered his bastle house for the queen and her party. As Michael came close, Sir Thomas jerked his chin. "Join us, sire. Bring your horses."

With a swirl of his cloak, Ferniehirst set off down the street towards the river, leading the ladies and Lord Livingston. Taking up the rear, Michael and the stable boy followed with the horses, and after a short distance they turned right down Smith's Wynd and found a large bastle house situated in an orchard beside the river.

"There are stables at the end of the orchard," Thomas jerked his chin at the stable boy. Then he opened his arm, indicating the impressive three-storey stone building ahead of them. "And this, Your Grace, is the house we built on the orders of your father, King James, when he wanted all rich landowners to build a fortified tower to help defend against the English." He gave a bow. "I place it at your disposal for the remainder of your visit, should you wish."

With William Livingston and Thomas Kerr to open the house for the queen and her ladies, and the stable boy to care for his horses, Michael felt superfluous, and offered to return to the inn to organise the transport of the queen's luggage.

At the Spread Eagle, to Michael's relief the fire seemed to

be mostly under control, with great clouds of black smoke billowing everywhere but little remaining evidence of flames.

Lord Seton caught sight of him and called him over. "Cranstoun! The fire seems to be contained now. Started behind the kitchens, so the landlord says. Can you show me where Ferniehirst has taken the queen?"

"Aye, of course." Michael gestured at the pile of luggage on the pavement. "Shall we take some of the queen's belongings wi' us?"

George shook his head. "I've sent a servant to fetch a cart. But I need to know where to send them."

Michael eyed the fourth floor of the building. "Could ye gie me a minute? I'll rescue my things, so I dinna smell o' smoke for the next week!"

Pushing past servants toiling down the stone stairs with kerchiefs wrapped around their mouths, Michael hurried up to his room and retrieved his saddlebag, throwing it over his shoulder, then rejoined Lord Seton. *I will need to find me some alternative lodgings for tonight.*

Back at the Kerr's bastle house, Michael and Seton found Sir Thomas in the first-floor banqueting hall, distributing rich red wine to the ladies. "Would you gentlemen like a glass?" he enquired as they entered. Then he noticed the saddlebag slung over Michael's shoulder. "And, Cranstoun, I know you were staying at the inn. Can I offer you a room at Ferniehirst for the night? 'Twill be full to overflowing here," he jerked his chin towards the crowd at the centre of the room, "but I have a small chamber you could use."

"My thanks," Michael gave a wry smile. "I should be able to get back to the inn on the morrow, but ye have saved me from a bed in the stables tonight!"

Sir Thomas handed Michael his wine with a quick nod of his head. "'Tis agreed, then."

They turned to the gathering in the main part of the room, where the queen and her maids sat chattering around the solid oak table that was the hall's centrepiece. The ladies were all talking at once, speculating as to the cause of the fire.

Lord Seton cleared his throat and bowed to the queen. "Your Grace, I will have the servants bring your belongings forthwith."

Sir Thomas pointed at the ceiling. "The queen can have the large bedroom above us, and her ladies the smaller rooms in the tower."

Seton nodded, and took his leave.

Taking a glass of wine from their host, Michael found that Flam had made a space for him between her and Beth.

"How are things at the inn?" she asked breathlessly. "Does the fire still rage? Do they know who started it?"

~

Cranstoun's answer was not what Mary expected, but it dispelled some of her worries.

"'Twas the bread the landlord was making for our breakfast," he said with a wry smile. "It started in the ovens."

So 'twas not the Protestant lords, after all. She had worried unnecessarily. But with the lords holding so much power—and hungry for more—a Catholic queen needed to be wary.

"But the damage hasnae been too extensive," Cranstoun continued. "If there's a good wind tomorrow, with the windows open to air the rooms, Your Grace should be able to return in a day or two."

Mary twirled the ruby ring on her little finger while she considered her options. This house had been designed for safety, it was big enough for her servants and trusted followers, and its build and position would make it harder for the lords of the congregation to attempt any wrongdoing.

She looked over at Ferniehirst. "Sir Thomas, if 'twould be convenient, I think I would prefer to stay 'ere while I am in Jedburgh."

CHAPTER 21

THURSDAY 10TH OCTOBER, 1566

AFTER A NIGHT at Ferniehirst Castle, Michael and Sir Thomas returned to the bastle house—which they had already started to call 'the queen's house'— the morning after the fire.

The day had dawned grey and dreich, and the heavy rain had dampened the ladies' enthusiasm for the trip to Stobs.

"Tomorrow!" insisted Flam. "We shall visit your castle on the morn. I am sure the sun will shine on us. But today you can join us here? This morning the queen is with her privy council. She issues edicts to the merchants of Jedburgh. Something about not raising their prices just because her court is in town. And then the assizes begin." She fluttered a hand in the direction of the tolbooth. "Very boring."

The Maries had been joined by a new maid, Libby Preston, a shy girl with silky fair hair and a curvaceous figure. Together they were good company for Thomas and Michael, sitting around the fire with their embroidery and whiling away the morning with games of piquet and gossip from court.

As a married man with an infant son, Sir Thomas got his

fair share of attention, but by the end of the morning, the ladies had acquainted themselves with many of the details of Michael's castle, lands and family tree. Those details that he was prepared to share with them...

He told them of his father and how he had died fighting the English at the Battle of Pinkie—but not of the much-loved older brother who had died in the same battle, leaving ten-year-old Michael as the sole heir of Stobs. He told them of his education in France—but not of the lonely years in Fontainebleau during which, unknown to him, his estate back in Scotland fell to ruin at the hands of marauding armies and a scurrilous steward. He told them of the strong tower house with its barmkin walls—but not of the many weeks he'd spent rebuilding the castle, stone by stone, after it was ravaged by the English. He told them of the tenants in their cottages—but not of the days he spent working along-side them, repairing dykes, planting and ploughing, to ensure his lands could provide some sort of a living to both them and him.

After hearing that he had no plans to marry—or none that he would admit to—Beth Beaton announced that the ladies would have to rectify that. "There are many young women—heiresses—who would be glad of your hand, Cranstoun. Why, there are some eligible heiresses in this very room," she said with a pointed look at Flam and Libby. "Or we can introduce you to others, if you would join us at court when we return to Edinburgh."

Her matchmaking looked to be getting rather out-of-hand, and Michael almost sighed with relief when he noticed the queen's terrier scratching at the door. "Ye must excuse me, ladies," he said, standing up, "The dog needs taken outside."

Flam pushed her chair back and hurried to the door with

him. "I shall come too. Jupiter might run off, since he doesn't know you very well."

And so, minutes later, Michael found himself in the orchard with Flam, both huddled under their cloaks against the persistent drizzle. Distant shouts and screeches from the marketplace echoed dully through the rain and acted as a counterpoint to the huffing of the dog, who carefully inspected—and baptised—every tree that they passed.

"The orchard was planted by the monks from the old abbey, so they say," said Flam. She stopped and tweaked an apple from a low-hanging bough. "And they've planted many varieties. This one," she took a bite from the rich red fruit, "is a Pippin. And that," she pointed at the next tree, "is a Monk's Pear. And, over there, a White Warden." She chuckled. "That one must've been planted to honour you."

Michael raised his eyebrows. "I wouldna have taken ye for a gardener."

Flam gave him a coquettish look. "There's much you don't know about me, sire. But when we were in France with the queen—before she came to Scotland—I was…" she hesitated, "*friends* with a French duke. He had vineyards in the Loire Valley, and would introduce me to the plants in the palace gardens." She stopped under a particularly large apple tree and looked up at him, her blue eyes flashing mischievously. "He also knew which shrubs were the best to hide a couple from prying eyes."

Looking behind them, Michael realised that they were, indeed, hidden from view down in this quiet corner of the orchard. "But you left this duke in France?"

With a lift of her shoulder, Flam pursed her lips. "When Francis, the queen's young husband, died, we—the Maries— vowed not to marry before the queen was ready to remarry. So the duke was not for me."

"But Mary is married to Darnley now. You could rekindle things with your duke?"

"Your concern is touching, sire, but he is wed now, with two children and a third on the way." She looked him in the eye. "And you should perchance be less noble? If you spend your days espousing the cause of others, you will never find yourself a rich heiress!" She tilted her chin and added softly, "Especially not one who has learned the ways of love in the courts of France."

With her face raised towards him, full lips slightly parted and her hand on his arm, she was almost asking to be kissed. And Michael, ever the gentleman, was sorely tempted to oblige. But even in this intimate moment with a beautiful woman who was obviously interested in him, a vision of Alexandra's tumbling raven locks and wide smile filled his mind and doused any attraction he felt for Flam.

There was something refreshing in the simplicity of Alexandra's wholesome looks and lack of artifice. In comparison, these courtly ladies might be beautiful, refined and clever, but they were more reminiscent of elegant lilies than unruly forget-me-nots.

Michael cleared his throat. "Methinks ye are too kind, my lady Fleming. The ladies of France would be sore disappointed by a lowly laird like me. Now," he turned back to the house and whistled for the dog, "we should return and get ourselves out of this infernal rain."

M asking her features so as not to show relief that the privy council was finally over, Mary dismissed her lords and withdrew to an ante-chamber where luncheon had been provided by the merchants of the town.

It had been a stormy morning, with the earl of Moray, as

usual, pushing for his favoured concerns and Mary stonewalling on many counts, especially when Moray's agendas related to further extending his power or were to the detriment of the old faith—as they often were.

Early in her reign, Moray, her half-brother, had been a valued adviser, giving strong counsel and wise direction. He had helped her, a French-raised Catholic woman, to win the grudging support of the majority of the Protestant lords.

But things had gone badly wrong when she had fallen in love with Lord Darnley.

The lords could not accept the Catholic Henry Stewart as her suitor, instead supporting the suit of Robert Dudley, Earl of Leicester and lover of the English queen, Elizabeth.

Having gained the support of the king of France, and blinded by love—or magic—Mary had defied them and married her cousin, whose lineage would add further strength to her claim for the English crown.

It was only afterwards that Mary began to wonder if her eyes had been clouded by enchantment rather than lust for her handsome swain. For Darnley's uncle, Ruthven, was said to be a sorcerer of the black arts. Could he have cast a spell, causing her to overlook the arrogance, vanity and selfishness exhibited by her young husband?

Those traits had made him many enemies at court, most notably Moray, who Darnley had accused of being too powerful and owning too much land.

Ever since, Moray's face had blackened any time he was forced into company with the king; but more often than not he absented himself on some flimsy excuse. Typically, he was also absent when Riccio had been murdered, although gossip had him as one of the plotters. And recently, word had reached Mary that Moray plotted with Elizabeth—also a Protestant—to set the Scottish crown upon his *own* head.

The fiercely royalist people of Scotland would not

support it, but Mary knew that the majority of her lords would support whichever side they thought would win, and they commanded large armies.

As was so often the case, the sovereign had to walk a narrow line, keeping favour with the lords by passing enough laws promoting their causes to keep them happy, whilst quietly backing other statutes to uphold her own interests.

All of this politicking had tired her, and she was glad of some food to recharge her energy before the assizes would start in the afternoon.

She hoped the court proceedings would give her a chance to assert her authority and show a strong hand by dispensing stiff penalties onto the miscreants that Bothwell and the Border lairds would bring before her. *Maybe then my lords will support me, rather than Moray,* she thought, knowing even as she did so that some of them were irredeemable.

The sweetness of some honeyed almonds had almost dissipated her sour mood when a messenger arrived and delivered a note that all but stopped her heart and threw her plans into disarray.

~

The afternoon brought a significant development which promised to elevate Michael's status and further delayed the ladies' proposed visit to Stobs.

Michael and Flam had not long returned from the orchard when a messenger arrived from the queen, requesting the presence of 'the deputy warden of the Middle March' at the tolbooth.

At Michael's questioning look, Sir Thomas gave an eloquent shrug. "Mayhap the Queen needs your knowledge of the Marches?"

And indeed, Ferniehirst proved somewhat correct. When Michael presented himself, rather nervously, to the queen, he discovered that the earl of Bothwell had been seriously injured while apprehending reivers at Hermitage, and Mary wished Michael to take his place, providing counsel as she presided over the assizes.

With her trusted Earl Huntly on her right, Michael was astonished to be shown into the seat to the left of the queen, between Her Grace and her secretary, Maitland; a position of such honour that he had to swallow hard and quell the racing of his heart as he sat down.

"You can advise me, Cranstoun," the Queen leaned towards him and whispered, "you know these Borderers better than I."

And so the next five days proceeded, Mary dispensing justice to the ruffians and villains brought before her, and earning Moray's displeasure by her leniency. The assizes were quieter than they might have been, due to the lack of Bothwell and his Liddesdale prisoners, but busy enough that Michael's days were full—and his evenings too, in the company of the queen and her ladies.

It was only in the mornings, when he quickly exercised Spirit, or at night when he tossed and turned in his room under the eaves of the Spread Eagle, that Michael's thoughts turned to his predicament.

His conversation with Flam in the orchard had disquieted him. *How will I ever marry if I can only think of an English-woman who is unavailable to me?* He had no answer to that. Try as he might to persuade himself that Flam was a better match, he could do no more than behave courteously to her, quietly deflecting her hints and flirtations, and waiting for the day when he could return to his quiet life at Stobs, free from the gossip and intrigue of the royal court.

CHAPTER 22

THE LADIES FINALLY got their visit to Stobs—a full week after it was originally suggested.

Six days of assizes were followed by a formal reception for Philibert Du Croc, the French ambassador, after which the queen announced that she wished to travel to Hermitage Castle on the morrow, to visit Bothwell on his sick bed and receive a briefing from him as governor of Liddesdale.

"You can be our guide, no?" she asked Michael, and of course he could not refuse.

"'Tis a long ride, ma'am," he replied. "I'd offer ye to stay overnight at Stobs, but sadly I havnae enough chambers to fit everyone."

Mary shook her head. "We will leave early in the morning and return the same day. After that we head for Duns—Libby wants us to visit Lord Home's castle where we will meet her mother."

Tapping a finger on the hilt of his sword, Michael did some quick calculations. "'Tis a ride of about five hours, if we keep a fair pace. Leaving at dawn we'd get to Hermitage around...midday." He glanced at the queen. "If a couple of hours would suffice for your business wi' Bothwell, we could be back to Jed in time for dinner. And," this time he caught Flam's eye, "we could stop at Stobs on the way, to break our fast."

~

The days and nights in their prison cell seemed interminably long. With nothing to do save talk, sleep, and eat the meagre rations provided three times a day—if they were lucky—Alex and Hob, already friends, became closer than ever.

They talked about their past escapades; about their hopes and dreams for the future; and about how they both missed their mothers. Hob's mother had been lost in a farming accident when he was just a youngster, and Alex's had died a few days after she'd been born.

From what she'd been told, her father's marriage to Cathy had been one of expediency rather than love, so he did not mourn his wife over long but threw himself back into the work of his lands and began to build a name for horse-breeding.

Never having known her mother, Alex did not grieve either. But when she saw the affection and interaction between her friends and their families, she knew that there was something missing from her life, and it made her sad.

Being brought up by a housekeeper, and with her father often away from home on clan business, Alex had unsurprisingly grown up independent and headstrong. But she got some of that family feeling from her friendship with Hob.

In their clan it was an open secret—known by everyone but never talked about—that Hob's mother had melted Iron Simon's heart not long after Cathy's death; and that Hob was almost certainly Alex's half-brother.

It was something they both knew but had never talked about until now, and somehow it brought them closer still. Of all their cold, dark days in the cell at Hermitage, it was one of the few good memories that Alex would retain. It was almost worth the deprivations and worry, for now she had someone she could call *brother*.

CHAPTER 23

T HE DAY OF their trip to Hermitage dawned grey and drizzly, putting a damper on the spirits of the group, and persuading all of the Maries, save Flam, that they would rather stay at home than face a long ride in inclement weather. However Libby Preston was not put off by the weather, so the queen had two ladies in attendance, plus a group of her lords, including Moray and Maitland, with Sir Thomas to aid Michael as the party's guide.

Their stop at Stobs was brief but long enough for Flam to appraise the tower and its outhouses.

In its secretive location, with a long approach through the narrow valley beside the Slitrig Water, the misty air gave the tower a sense of mystery and otherworldliness.

But no amount of romance or fantasy could make Michael's keep into an impressive castle on the scale of Edinburgh or Stirling, and he detected some disappointment in Flam's demeanour.

She had flirted with him less since that day in the garden at Jedburgh, and for the rest of their journey to Hermitage, she rode with William Maitland, the queen's grey old secretary who had little to commend him save the grand castle of Lethington, near Haddington.

Michael kept his thoughts to himself, but this was a development he was glad of, for Flam's sake as well as his own.

～

At Mary's first sight of Hermitage Castle, she pulled her white palfrey to a halt, swallowing hard. She saw now why this keep had such a fearsome reputation and why her grandfather, James IV, had taken it under the control of the crown. For whoever owned this formidable fortress would be virtually unassailable, and if it fell into the hands of the English—as it nearly had, in her grandfather's time—this part of the Borders could easily pass to enemy control.

I am glad Lord Bothwell is trustworthy. He had proven himself a staunch supporter of both Mary and her mother, when she was regent, on many occasions. *But if he ever deserts me...* Mary took a deep breath. She would just need to keep him happy and keep him loyal.

～

A jangling of keys at their cell door wakened Alex from dreams of a blond-haired laird sitting in sunny meadow, picking daisies and twining them into her hair.

Reluctantly, she opened her eyes to the light of day and a reality that had more in common with nightmares—cold, hungry and captured by a notorious earl.

Rubbing her eyes, she sat up stiffly then ducked as some objects came flying towards her and Hob.

"Git yer boots on and come 'ere," said a guard who

smelled as bad as she and Hob must, after over a week in Bothwell's prison.

Stuffing cold feet into her boots, Alex hobbled to the door, only to have her arms pinned roughly behind her back and her hands tied tightly at the wrists.

Beside her, a second guard tied Hob's hands, then the first commanded, "Follow me," and set off down the spiral staircase.

Hob caught her eye, his cheeks hollow and his freckles invisible under a layer of grime. He looked as worried as she felt. But they had no option but to fall in behind the heavily armed guard, following him down the stone steps and across the main court of the castle.

Alex chewed her lip, her stomach churning with worry about what fate might bring them next. Was the earl about to 'interview' her again? *Or worse?*

CHAPTER 24

ALEX STOOD IN the great hall of Hermitage once more, her heart in her mouth.

Again she faced the earl of Bothwell, but this time he was not alone, and there was no sign of his shrewish wife.

Instead, he sat swathed in bandages on a padded chair in pride of place beside a woman who could only be the queen of Scots, surrounded by a retinue of lords and courtiers. Resplendent in their velvets and jewels, the nobles reminded Alex of richly-hued peacocks and iridescent ravens—but they were very out-of place in this grey, colourless castle.

Alex felt out of place too; tired, dirty and malodorous after more than a week in the prison tower. But with Hob standing resolutely beside her, she took some small comfort from his presence. However, things didn't bode well; not with the might of Scotland ready to judge them and her nemesis, the earl, part of the jury.

Bothwell flicked a finger at the captives. "English reivers, ma'am. Caught them taking a horse from the Armstrongs."

"Not taking, *retrieving*," Alex burst out, heedless of protocol. If her hands hadn't been tied, she'd have put them defiantly on her hips. Instead she shook off her weakness and fatigue and stood tall and proud. "The Armstrongs had stolen Duke from our keep." She turned hot eyes on Bothwell. "We were on a *trod*."

"So you say," retorted the earl, "but *I* say that you saw the Armstrongs with a valuable stallion and, as an unrepentant reiver, decided you'd have him for yourself."

Bothwell's reply was like a slap to the face, and Alex had to steel herself to stop from reeling at his words. And then a movement behind the queen caught her eye, and her mouth fell open in surprise.

Leaning over and whispering into the queen's ear was *Michael*, the last person she'd have thought to see here. But thoughts of those blue eyes, his kind smile and that glorious golden hair had sustained her during many a dark hour in the prison tower, and she would recognise him anywhere.

She was still recovering from the shock of seeing him here when she spotted the beautiful brunette who stood beside him, with a smile dimpling her cheeks and her gaze fastened adoringly on Michael.

The bottom fell out of Alex's world.

Michael had a—*wife*?

~

It was the first time Michael had ever been inside Hermitage Castle, and he hoped that it might be the last. Even with a fire crackling in the oversized hearth and thick tapestries hanging on the walls, it was a dank, soulless place that sapped at his energy and made his skin crawl.

Mayhap it was the reputation the castle had—there were stories of its wicked first laird being boiled in lead by his servants, an enemy English baron drowning in suspicious circumstances in a deep pool, or an early owner starving a rival to death in the vile dungeons. And of course, the current incumbent, James Hepburn, was notoriously ambitious and cruel, even if loyal to Queen Mary.

'Tis not a place I want to tarry in, Michael thought with a shiver, as the guards brought in the first prisoners and everyone turned their attention to the open space at the centre of the great hall.

But when the two miscreants were pushed into the makeshift courtroom, Michael thought for a moment that his eyes deceived him; that he was now hallucinating about the Englishwoman as well as dreaming about her every night. However, as soon as she jutted her chin and contradicted the earl with her usual fearless spirit, he knew that it was Alexandra. *His* Alexandra. Bone-thin, grimy and dishevelled, yet still enchanting.

He had no idea how the Englishwoman had ended up in Bothwell's prison, and he hoped for her sake that the dungeons weren't as gruesome as he had heard, but he was sure that she told the truth. If the Armstrongs had somehow got hold of Duke, then *of course* she would try to rescue him. He would have done the same for Mist. And probably Spirit too, now that he had got to know the new horse better.

Michael cleared his throat, and it had the desired effect.

The queen's head tilted in his direction. "You 'ave something to say, Cranstoun?" she murmured.

He inclined his head. "Aye, Your Grace."

The queen lifted a hand, silencing Bothwell—and Alexandra too, surprisingly. "My Lord Cranstoun wishes to speak."

Michael stepped forward, wetting lips that had suddenly gone dry. "My Lord Bothwell, there is an easy way to prove this woman's claim." He opened an arm, indicating Alexandra and Hob. "Bring the horse here, and let the girl ride it. Then let one of the duke's men ride it, and see who has the mastery of the beast."

"No!" Alexandra cried out, and every eye turned in her direction again. "Let this man be the rider." She jerked her chin at Michael. "And I should ride second, lest he divines my methods or signals."

"That would be more fair, I think," said the queen. "Cranstoun is a skilled rider." She turned to Bothwell. "Have your men saddle the horse and bring it..." she paused a moment, her brow wrinkling, "to the courtyard below. The portcullis should deter any ideas of escape."

~

H is heart in his mouth, Michael mounted the black stallion, with a crowd of curious onlookers scrutinising his every move.

Nudging Duke forward, Michael walked him around the makeshift arena, remembering Alexandra's cautions not to be too forceful with his commands. *I have to be quick. And make this look good. But not too good.* He needed to live up to the queen's belief in him, but leave room for the English-woman to dance and trick with the horse, as he knew she could.

He glanced behind him, wondering where Alexandra had got to, and at that slight change in his balance, Duke's shoulders swung around, and he ended up facing the other direction. Michael clenched his teeth, then gave the queen a small bow. *Pretend you meant that.* Then he urged the horse forward again, thinking to trot a circle, then canter, and leave it at that.

But it seemed Duke could read his mind. For rather than walking sedately around the circle, the horse took one step and then skipped into a slow canter, his shoulders light and his stride so comfortable it felt like riding on air.

For half a circuit Michael just sat there, unable to stop a grin spreading across his face. When they'd been escaping the Armstrongs, he'd not really had the chance to appreciate how remarkable this horse was. But now that he could properly appreciate riding him, he understood how Alexandra would risk the Armstrongs and Bothwell's prison in order to rescue him. He was an aristocrat among equines. A true Duke.

Passing opposite the stairs to the Douglas Tower, Michael finally spotted Alexandra on the other side of the ring. Without meaning to, he turned slightly towards her—and Duke took that as another signal. Suddenly he was pirouetting, almost on the spot, his shoulders skipping a yard or so with every stride whilst his hindquarters bounced around in a tiny circle.

Michael almost laughed at the absurdity of it. Without meaning to, he had made the horse dance. *But I must stop, or there will be nothing left for Alexandra to show.*

Once again, his thought was Duke's command. With a graceful 'one-two' of his front feet, the horse halted, happening to end up facing the queen.

Michael thought quickly and swept the bonnet from his head, bowing as deeply as he could manage from atop the black stallion, before leaping off.

The queen quirked an eyebrow. "Very impressive, Cranstoun."

Michael patted Duke's shoulder. "This horse has been very well trained."

"Indeed," Mary replied. "Now, let us see the prisoner ride him."

With that, Alexandra was pushed forward, rubbing her

wrists where they'd been untied, her eyes blazing furiously at Michael.

His heart sinking, Michael realised that he must've made too good a show. He swallowed. *How can I make it up to her?* And then inspiration struck.

"Let me adjust the stirrups for you, my lady," he said, giving Alexandra a significant look then turning to adjust Duke's saddle. "I'm sure you will need your stirrups set right to ride this fine beast."

She took the hint. "No." Her nostrils flared. "Remove the saddle," she said imperiously, and a mutter went around the crowd. "And the bridle," she added, and this time there was an audible gasp from the onlookers.

Alex gave her hands a shake to ensure that they worked properly after being tied so tightly. Then she circled her shoulders gingerly, testing how well her broken bone had knitted, and faced Duke.

It felt so good to see the horse again, and she had enjoyed watching Michael ride him, even if she was upset about his wife and annoyed because he'd ridden better than she had hoped. *But that is why you like him,* she told herself. *Liked him,* she corrected. *Because he rides well and wants to ride better.*

Michael took a step towards her, to leg her up onto Duke, and caught her eye. The intensity of his stare made her heart beat faster, and she had to make a conscious effort to break his gaze before anyone watching would suspect that they knew one another, or that she felt anything towards him. For in this evil earl's lair, with Michael's wife standing nearby, that could be fatal—for both of them.

But that one look, and the effect he had on her pulse and her emotions, was enough to remind her that she didn't just like him because of his skill on a horse. *But I must put that behind me. He is not for me.*

As Michael boosted her onto the horse, he gave her calf a quick squeeze of reassurance, a signal that would be invisible to the onlookers, but helped calm her nerves, even as it confused her emotions. Had he been married, those few days ago when he kissed her so passionately? He didn't seem the type to cheat on a wife—and especially one so beautiful as the maid beside the queen. He was an enigma.

Taking a moment to settle herself on Duke's back, Alex took a deep breath and tried to clear her mind of thoughts of Michael, for that would not help her now. She focussed her attention on the horse, sat tall, then gave the tiny nudge with her calves that would send him forwards.

After a week of inactivity and hunger in prison, her muscles were not as strong as they should be, and her shoulder was still damaged, so she would need to keep this display short—but impressive.

With a nudge of her knee, she gave Duke the signal to start 'Spanish walk', and the impressive and imperious lift of each foreleg in turn raised a murmur of awe in the watching crowd.

Turning across the centre, Alex halted Duke in front of the queen, then lifted her weight slightly until he started to walk backwards. Once he'd gone far enough, she stopped him, then mimed a curtsey, before sending him forward into the hovering trot the Italians called 'passage'. After one circuit, she slowed him until he was trotting on the spot. In piaffe, she pirouetted him until he faced the other way, and then nudged him into canter.

Michael had already stolen her thunder by performing a canter pirouette, so instead she made Duke perform 'flying changes' every second stride, which made him skip along as if he were dancing.

This was more taxing on her muscles and energy, and after one circle she had to slow Duke to a walk and then stopped, again in front of the queen. Heart in her mouth, she gave a command she'd only ever practised from the ground, hoping that Duke would remember what to do, even without her standing in front of him and pointing.

"Bow!" she said, and, after a moment's hesitation, Duke bent and lifted a foreleg, leaning his neck and head towards the ground.

Alex used the momentum of his movement to throw her leg over his neck and slide to the ground, landing on her feet beside his shoulder, where she, too, bowed deeply to the queen.

Rising from her bow, she felt a moment's trepidation. *Did I do enough?* It was not only her own fate that depended on this, but also that of Hob, Duke, and their other two horses. And as heiress to Kersdale, the fate of her family name depended on her too.

CHAPTER 25

MICHAEL LET OUT a deep breath as Alexandra finished her dramatic display and bowed to the queen, hoping that it was not only he who had been impressed.

But he need not have worried. The queen's face was wreathed in smiles, and she clapped her hands in delight. At this signal, the lords and ladies surrounding her burst into applause.

As Alexandra stood up from her bow, for a moment she looked bewildered at the reaction, and then she blanched, and her legs began to give way.

In a heartbeat, Michael leapt forward and grabbed her around the waist. He looked angrily at Bothwell. "When did you last feed these prisoners? This woman faints from lack of nourishment."

Bothwell had the grace to look embarrassed, but the queen forestalled his answer.

"Call the boy over," she commanded, "and bring some water for the girl."

Someone pulled a wooden chair over, and Michael

lowered Alexandra into it, handing her the pewter cup a servant had produced. Then he busied himself putting the bridle back onto Duke.

By this time Hob stood before the queen, his knees visibly trembling inside his thin trews.

"What is your name, boy?" Mary asked.

"Hob Forster, Your Majesty."

"Your Grace," hissed Michael. "We say 'Your Grace' in Scotland."

"Sorry ma'am, I mean, Your Grace." Hob looked chastened.

"And the girl's name?"

"Alexandra Graham. Daughter of Simon and heiress of Kersdale."

At this last answer, Michael frowned. He knew Simon was Alexandra's father, but she had never said anything about being his heir. Were there no brothers? He glanced at her but she was drinking thirstily.

The queen tilted her head at Hob. "And when did you last eat?"

Hob took a moment to answer this one, his forehead creasing and his eyes rolling skywards as if thinking hard. "Maybe two days ago." He shrugged and rubbed his belly. "Or three."

A muscle twitched in the queen's jaw, and after a moment's contemplation she addressed Michael. "Do these Grahams of Kersdale cause trouble in the Marches, Cranstoun?"

Michael shook his head. "Not that I know of, Your Grace."

Mary pressed her lips together, then she sat tall and put her hands on the arms of her chair. "Alexandra of Kersdale, I find you and 'ob Forster blameless against the accusation of reiving. You are 'ereby pardoned, and may, if you wish, return to your clan. You shall be recompensed with ten gold coins each, and you will dine here momentarily, to regain your strength. But," and here she looked directly at Alexandra, "should you wish, I would have you work for me. I would give you a position in my household as Riding Master."

~

Alex blinked at the queen, not trusting her ears. "Riding master?" she repeated, sure she must've misunderstood.

"Yes," replied the queen. "You will teach me and my ladies —and my young son when 'e is grown—to ride like that. Train our horses. You shall 'ave an 'ouse in Edinburgh, so you are close at 'and."

"But she is an Englishwoman!" Bothwell's gruff voice interjected, and he pointed at her accusingly, his hand heavily bandaged. "You cannot trust the English, ma'am. She could be a spy for Elizabeth—or be an assassin!"

~

Michael glanced at Alexandra and saw how her shoulders tightened under the earl's gaze. *Something has gone on there.* And, knowing Bothwell's reputation, it could well have been against her will. A kernel of anger stirred in his stomach. *I must get her away from this blackguard.*

He stepped forward. "My Lord Bothwell, is it nae true that this lady was imprisoned in your dungeons for pursuing the thieves who took her horse?" He opened his hands. "So it's hardly likely she's a spy or an assassin. She wasnae anywhere near Jedburgh or the queen."

Bothwell glared at Michael. "Maybe so. But she set fire to

the tower at Mangerton, and the Armstrongs are subjects of Her Grace."

"Which is exactly what they did to *our* bastle house!" interjected Alexandra. "They burned our winter stocks of hay, and now our animals will starve, for 'tis long past harvest."

Mary held up a hand. "It seems there was fault on both sides. But," she addressed herself to Alexandra, "if you are to be part of my 'ousehold, we need some guarantee of your good behaviour."

Alexandra frowned, for once at a loss for words.

"Hah! You can't trust an English reiver. They never change." For a man that had been reported to be on his deathbed, Bothwell's arguments were remarkably vigorous.

The earl's attitude reveals more about him than about Alexandra. But she was still in danger from Bothwell, who seemed to have some sort of grievance against her, and he was not known to give up on a grudge.

Michael needed to stop this argument and get Alexandra away from Bothwell. But maybe there was a way; something he had done before, at the day of truce...

He stepped forward. "Your Grace, if it please you, I will attest to her good behaviour on my honour as deputy warden."

"But why would you do that? She is nothing to you," Bothwell cut in.

Michael bristled at the contempt in the earl's tone. But he was right. Turnbull had been Michael's tenant, so he had a reason to speak for the man. However, as far as all here knew, Alexandra meant nothing to him.

Before Michael could reply, Bothwell continued, his eyes glittering malevolently. "Or do you wish her to *be* something to you?" He jerked his chin. "You would be better with another, not this frigid English vixen."

His jaw clenching, Michael's hand slid to his sword hilt. *That man is a knave.*

"Cranstoun!" The queen's voice was sharp, and it snapped his attention from the earl back to her. "The lady is an heiress," she raised a questioning eyebrow, and gave him a knowing look, "about which we 'ave 'ad discussions. Per'aps there is a way to benefit you both. Would you take this woman?"

It took a moment for the queen's meaning to find its way past Michael's anger at the earl. "You mean...?" *Marry her?*

CHAPTER 26

A LEX PUSHED HERSELF out of the chair, and addressed herself to nobody in particular. "Do *I* not get a say in this? Before I even decide to accept the queen's offer, you would betroth me—to a man who already has a wife!" She glared accusingly at the brunette maid. "Mayhap you Scots are as uncouth as they say, but *I* will not marry a bigamist!"

There was a stunned silence, and then the queen tilted her head at Michael. "You have a wife, Cranstoun?"

Michael's face had gone white, and he turned hurt eyes on Alex. "Why would ye say that? I'm nae married. Never have been."

"But..." Alex eyed the brunette again, realising that she had, as usual, jumped to conclusions, and that she must've been wrong. *I need to learn not to make assumptions.* Perhaps this maid just dreamed of Michael, as she had. With looks like his, he must have many admirers.

She cast her eyes downwards. "My apologies, sire. Mayhap I misread things."

"So," Mary looked from Alex to Michael and back again.

"What say you? Work as my Riding Master, and marry laird Cranstoun?"

Before Alex could find the words to reply, Michael shook his head. "We canna marry, Your Grace. She is English; I am Scots. 'Tis forbidden."

Alex's heart sank. *He does not wish to marry me.* But even as that realisation made her shoulders slump and her eyes sting, she recognised that her disappointment answered the queen's second question—she *would* have married Michael, if only he would have her.

She might hardly know him, but she knew the important things—that he was kind, loyal and caring; attributes that any woman would be glad to have in a husband. And attributes that had been missing in all the potential suitors her father had paraded before her.

The queen obviously trusted Michael, and had he not said that he was deputy warden? *He kept that a secret from me!* She remembered his mirth that first day at the meadow when she'd threatened to report him to the warden. No wonder he had laughed! Her mouth curled at the memory, despite her dismay that he would not have her.

∽

M ary looked from Cranstoun to the English girl. *Something goes on there.* They were both visibly upset at the idea they could not marry. She had an inkling that this was not the first time they'd met. But there was obviously some bad blood between Bothwell and the girl, so, whatever happened, Alexandra would be better away from Hermitage.

Catching Cranstoun's eye, Mary inclined her head. "You are correct, Cranstoun. Under Scots law, you cannot marry an English woman. But," she held up a finger, "as sovereign, I can grant a licence for you to wed, should you so wish."

The laird's eyes widened, then he turned to the girl. "What say you, Alexandra? Would you marry me, as bond for your good behaviour? And would you ride for the queen?"

~

Heart in his mouth, Michael waited for Alexandra's reply. Around him, the restless nobles had stilled, all eyes fixed on the drama playing out in the centre of the courtyard.

Hazel eyes flashing, Alexandra squared her shoulders under her grubby chemise. "Your proposal sounds more like a business arrangement. A lady would have her betrothal be more...romantic."

Michael looked around him theatrically and shrugged. "'Tis difficult to be romantic with such an audience."

~

Inwardly, Alex smiled at Michael's dramatics. But she could not let him win her so easily and kept her face stern while she considered whether to push him for more.

Hob Forster had been quiet throughout this playful exchange, his eyes growing wider and frown deeper with each counter argument. At Michael's last comment, he piped up, "But you mayn't marry, Alex! Not wi'out your father's say-so."

Alexandra's good spirits fled, leaving only a hollow feeling where happiness had been brewing. *Father! He will never allow it!* "He's right," she said, glancing first at the queen and then Michael. "I'm his only child. Any union would need his blessing. And you are a Scot, sire. He will mislike that."

Tapping a finger on the arm of her chair, the queen was silent for a moment. Then a smile wreathed her face. "I 'ave it!" She pointed at both of them. "An 'andfasting. A contract that will bind you, Alexandra of Kersdale, to Michael of Stobs, and 'e to you. Terms that should allay my Lord Bothwell's concerns for my security. But the betrothal will give time for us to speak with your father, and set things right before you marry. He may mislike it less if the queen suggests it. What say you?"

CHAPTER 27

PICKING AT THE cuff of his jerkin, Michael tried to ignore the queasy feeling in his stomach. When this day started, his only concern had been to get the queen safely to Hermitage and back again to Jedburgh. Who would have thought it would have turned out like this?

The queen caught his eye. "You are ready, Cranstoun?" she murmured.

"Aye."

"And you are sure?"

He paused for a moment, then nodded. "Aye." There had been something about Alexandra from the moment he had first seen her—when he had thought she was a lad. Something about her that made him care about what she thought and what she did, and made him want to keep her safe. Which was what he was doing now—keeping her safe from Bothwell and anyone who would accuse her because she was not a Scot.

"You know that you could 'ave married one of my ladies, 'ad you wished?" Mary said, casting her eyes at the other side of the room, where Flam stood in a huddle with some of the other courtiers. "One with a fine dowry and a title to share. You still could."

This question requires a careful answer or I could cause offence. "I wouldnae ha' presumed myself worthy of any of the ladies who attend you, Your Grace." He glanced at the door to the upper chambers. "This Alexandra of Kersdale will suit better. And," he brushed at his sleeve again, "'tis a hand-fasting. An agreement to marry. If she does not wish to stay wi' me, or her father will not allow, we can break the agreement."

The queen nodded slowly, the pearls of her headdress glowing palely in the flickering lights from the candles illuminating the hall. But whatever she would have said next was lost, as the tower door opened, and a vision in cramoisie and white entered.

Alexandra. But Alexandra as he'd never seen her before— with her hair cleaned and curling softly around her shoulders, jewels around her neck and her fine figure accentuated by the cut of the borrowed gown she wore. She looked like a goddess descended to the mortal world from the heights of Mount Venus; far too beautiful for surroundings like this or a man like him.

All Michael's worries faded away. *How came I to deserve an angel like this?*

~

This last hour of Alex's life must surely qualify as one of the strangest she had ever lived through. From a rank prison cell, to dancing with her horse in front of the queen of Scots, to being offered employment in the royal household— the kind of position she had only dreamed of—to a proposal from the man who had filled her dreams for the last weeks. *Mayhap I am still dreaming?* She pinched herself. *No.*

And now, standing at the entrance to the great hall, her

life was about to change irrevocably. Clean, fragrant and dressed like a lady, thanks to the ministrations of Jean Gordon and Libby Preston, she would leave this place betrothed to a man she hardly knew and live in a country she had heretofore only visited to reive or train her horse.

But one glance at Michael and any misgivings she might have had disappeared like snow off a dyke. Catching her eye, his smile lit the room, and took the breath from her lungs.

In a few steps she was by his side, facing the queen of Scots.

With a few words, Mary outlined their purpose and asked them to join hands to signify the joining of their lives.

After a few heartbeats, they were gazing into each others' eyes, their hands wrapped together with a golden cord.

With only an imperceptible tremor in his voice, Michael gave his vow. "Alexandra Graham of Kersdale, to thee I plight my troth, to give my hand in marriage until death us do part."

No mention of love. But perhaps that was not a surprise, given that they hardly knew each other and nobody present knew they'd even met before today. Love could grow, she knew, given the right ingredients. And this gloriously handsome, kind and strong man had all the right attributes to light a fire in her belly. If she could do the same for him, it would surely lead to love? *Maybe not today, or tomorrow, but sometime soon.*

She lifted her chin. "Michael Cranstoun of Stobs, to thee I plight my troth..."

CHAPTER 28

LEAVING HERMITAGE WITH Alexandra by his side, Michael's heart was lighter than it had been before. They still had obstacles to overcome, and a relationship to build, but they had forever to do that—if only her father would say yes.

Hob Forster had been dispatched to Kersdale with a letter from the queen asking Simon Graham to join them in Jedburgh as soon as was convenient, and a passport giving him safe passage to do so.

Given Michael's last experience of Simon—being accused of spying, then escaping from his barn—he didn't expect a warm reception from the English laird. But the queen of Scots was charming and gracious, and Michael felt sure she would be able to smooth the way for their marriage.

"Alexandra," he glanced across to where she rode beside him, "there's a tailor in Jed if ye want to get another dress made for the wedding." He pointed at the simpler clothes she'd borrowed to ride in. "And other day clothes if ye wish. I have money I can gie ye."

Pursing her lips, she grinned impishly. "And I have ten

gold coins from the queen. I can buy my own dress, sire. But thank you for the consideration."

"As ye wish."

Turning off the westward path from Hermitage, and leading their band of lords and ladies onto the old drove road that led northwards beside the Braidley Burn, a hare skittered off the track ahead of them. Grey skies hung low overhead; the tops of hills like Cauldcleuch Head buried in low cloud. Michael pulled his cloak over his head against the persistent mizzle, his nostrils filling with the bitter scent of bracken as Spirit's hooves thudded hollowly on the peaty ground.

Pondering their upcoming nuptials, a dreadful thought occurred to him. "I never asked before. Ye *are* a Catholic? Or do I need to find one of those followers of Knox for a Protestant service?"

She laughed out loud at that. "That would be a fine mess, if I were a reformist. But no, we Grahams still follow the old religion."

I have so much to learn about this woman. He smiled back at her. *But there will be time, provided we can persuade Iron Simon.* "And after we are wed, would ye want some days in Jed for a honeymoon? Or shall we just retire straight back to Stobs?" He gave her a lopsided grin. "There's a big, comfortable, feather mattress and a warm fire in my chamber."

Her brow wrinkled. "Stobs? But I'll be staying in Edinburgh, so that I can ride for the queen."

"But—my lands are at Stobs. My tenants. My work..." At her stony look he tailed off.

"I only agreed to marry because of the queen's offer of work. All the suitors father could suggest wanted me to be a brood mare, producing youngsters and keeping house. But I want *more* from life," she added passionately. "If I cannot work for the queen, then we cannot marry."

Michael shook his head. "Stobs is too far to ride to Edinburgh and back in a day, and still hae time for work." He pointed at Duke. "And your horse would soon wear out, travelling all those miles."

"I will have to live somewhere else then. Somewhere nearer."

With a sigh, Michael raised his shoulders. "And I canna afford to rent us somewhere nearer. The estate makes little enough as it is."

She glared at him. "I thought you were a laird."

"Aye. But the English razed our lands and father died in battle while I was still a boy. Stobs was ruined when I took it over. It's only these last few years it's begun to turn a profit."

"Well, I can't stay in Stobs if I'm to work for the queen." Her eyes dropped to the gold hand-fasting cord, which she'd tied around her wrist like a bracelet.

"But ye'll have to stay in Stobs when ye're married to me."

She swallowed hard, then turned to look at him, her eyes glistening. "Then I can't marry you. I need to be my own woman. I want to work for the queen."

~

Mary frowned. *Something is wrong with those two.* At the beginning of the ride Cranstoun and the girl had laughed and joked together, but something had changed, and for the last mile they had ridden in stony silence, leading the group along Braidley Burn to the turnoff at Crib Burn, and now up the steep narrow cleft beside the stream as it led to Swire Knowe.

As the one to suggest the hand-fasting, Mary felt a responsibility for the couple, for she had been a matchmaker of sorts. Seeing them estranged like this was too reminiscent of her own early days with Darnley—and that was not a good example to follow. *Mayhap I can smooth over whatever ails them.* Pushing her horse past her ladies, she made to catch up with Michael and Alexandra.

But Mary had not reckoned on the slippery ground. On this steeper section of the hill, the path narrowed, and as she urged him forward, her white palfrey lost his footing. With a scrabble and a grunt, his hindquarters lurched and he began to topple sideways.

With a cry of alarm, Mary was thrown from the saddle, instinctively kicking her feet to free them from the stirrups before she would be trapped underneath him.

All the breath was knocked from her lungs as she landed on the—thankfully soft—ground, but a glance to her left showed that the horse was still sliding, and might crush her. Rolling further away, she spun herself out of reach—and into greater danger. For there was no longer soft ground underneath her, but only a dank quagmire that trapped her in its filthy grip.

In seconds her clothes were soaked by the icy black mud that surrounded her and sucked her inexorably into the foul depths of the bog.

"Help!" she cried, struggling to heave herself out of the mire. But it was useless. As much as she attempted to pull herself forwards, the mud sucked her further under, the heavy skirts of her riding suit dragging her down and making the situation worse.

Is this what it has come to? Had she survived the machinations of her rebel lords, a difficult childbirth and the assassination of her secretary, only to lose her life on this godforsaken Borders hillside?

Sending up a silent prayer, she stopped struggling and composed herself. *I am in God's hands now. If it is His will, He will save me.*

CHAPTER 29

ALEX's MIND WAS in turmoil as they traversed the steep hill. Her heart warred with her ambition; her desire to be her own woman and seek her destiny as a horse trainer warring with her desire for Michael. For, of all the men she had ever met, he was the only one to touch her emotions and kindle a fire in her belly.

But if they could not reconcile this issue of where to live, how could they be together? She could see no way forward, and it blackened her mood.

A commotion behind roused Alex from her introspection. Glancing over her shoulder, her heart leapt into her mouth at the sight of the queen tumbling down the hill, with her palfrey scrabbling on his back as he slid after her, trying to right himself.

Throwing herself off Duke, Alex raced down the bank to where the queen had fallen. When she hit the edge of the bog Alex stopped short.

Ahead of her, Mary floundered in the mud, her face a mask of fear and panic.

"Lie still!" Alex commanded. "Spread your arms." Casting

her eyes around the hillside, she looked frantically for a long branch or other implement they could use to reach the queen. But on this barren moorland there was nothing save bracken and grass.

Pulling off her boots, she tossed them behind her. Lying on the wet grass, she shimmied forward cautiously as Michael slid to a stop beside her. "Hold my feet," she threw over her shoulder.

Michael's big hands gripped her ankles, but he tried to pull her back. "Let me go, lass. I'm stronger."

"And heavier. You'll sink easier," she gasped as the cold mud hit her skin.

A few yards in front of her, the queen was sinking, her eyes wide and her mouth moving silently. She'd spread her arms, as Alex had said, but she was being sucked quickly into the bog, an inch at a time. It was past her waist now, and when it got to her shoulders Alex's job would be almost impossible.

Spreading her body as wide as she could, she slithered forward until she felt Michael's grip tighten. "I canna go any further, lass, I'm sinking too."

We're close. So close. The queen's hand was only inches away. *If only I had something to throw.* A rope. A... With a cry of triumph, she remembered the cord on her wrist.

The mud was up to the queen's chest now; there was not much time left. But the act of untying the cord from her wrist had been enough to make Alex sink a little too. She needed to save Mary quickly, or both of them would die.

"Your Grace!" Alex got the queen's attention. "Catch this, and hold tight." She quickly fashioned a knot in the end, then cast the rope at the queen. But it curled in the air and fell into the black bog. With a groan of frustration, Alex pulled it back and tried again. This time, the extra weight of mud helped the cord to fly truer, and it landed near the queen's hand.

Mary reached for the rope as she sank to her armpits in the bog.

"Hold on," Alex said, knotting the other end of the cord around her good wrist. "Michael, pull!"

At her command, a steady pressure started on her ankles, and she was dragged slowly backwards. After only a few inches, the rope pulled taut, and progress slowed. "Be strong, Mary," she said, forgetting protocol in her worry. Because the strength—or otherwise—of the queen would determine whether they could save her.

Other hands had joined Michael, and the pressure on her ankles grew. "Not too much!" she shouted in alarm. "Slowly, so the queen can hold on."

They must've heeded her warning, as the drag became more slow and steady, and Alex almost cried with relief to see the sodden lace of Mary's chemise poking through the mud.

Mary grasped the cord with her other arm, risking sinking further so she'd have a better grip.

"Pull again," Alex commanded, ignoring the pain where the cord dug into her skin, already raw from Bothwell's bonds.

But their rescuers were over-eager, and their latest efforts were so strong that they pulled the cord right out of Mary's hands.

Michael watched in horror as Alexandra and the Queen slid further apart, and the queen began sinking again.

"No!" Alexandra shimmied forward like a lizard, and this

time she was able to grab the queen's hands. "Now!" she shouted back at the men. "But slowly. Our grip is slippery."

Inch by inch, he and Sir Thomas—who had joined him and held Alexandra's left ankle—pulled the ladies out of the bog. It seemed to take forever, and by the end of it they were all muddy and exhausted, sitting in an unceremonious heap on the rough grass at the edge of the bog.

"My thanks," the queen gasped, her teeth chattering.

Sir Thomas swept off his cloak and wrapped it around the queen. "We need to get you warm, ma'am." The queen was hustled to the side, attended to by Flam, Maitland and Libby.

Alexandra was almost as muddy as the queen, and Michael's cloak was soaked too. While Ferniehirst rustled up some more dry cloaks from amongst the lords, Michael retrieved Alex's boots as she wiped her feet on the rough grass.

"D'ye feel up to riding?" he asked.

She nodded, looking over at the queen, who was in worse shape. Absent-mindedly, Alexandra re-wrapped the gold cord around her wrist, tying it carefully.

Does she still care? Michael wondered. She had saved the cord after their hand-fasting, and now she saved it again, even though ruined. Could they put their argument behind them and find a way forward? He hoped so. Despite their differences, there was a lot to tie them together, not least the cord around her wrist.

～

On her feet once more, Alex's eye was drawn by the queen's palfrey, who was being led back to the path by Huntly. Covered in black mud and slime so there was little of his white coat visible, the horse limped noticeably.

Assisted by Maitland, the Queen approached and grasped Alexandra's hands. "You saved my life," she started to say, and then shivered violently. Her hair was plastered in mud, as were her underclothes.

"We need to get you moving, ma'am," Flam said, pulling the cloak tighter around the queen's shoulders, "and into some dry clothes."

Michael jerked his chin northwards. "We should ride for Stobs with all haste. I will send word to get hot baths prepared—and fresh clothes."

"But the queen's horse is lame." Alex pointed at the palfrey, who now stood resting a hind leg. She turned to the queen. "You can ride Duke, ma'am. He will keep you safe."

Mary inclined her head. "I would be 'onoured."

Taking Alex's elbow, Michael gave her a sideways look. "Ye can ride wi' me then. Spirit is strong enough to take two." Then he caught Ferniehirst's eye. "Sir Thomas, would ye ride ahead to Stobs and ask Mrs Beattie to prepare two baths? Ye know the way, do ye not?"

Ferniehirst nodded. "I would be glad to." Hurrying off, he mounted quickly and galloped away up the glen.

The rest of the party also made their way to the horses, leading them onto flatter, dryer, ground before climbing aboard and following at a warming trot.

At the head of the group, and with the persistent drizzle on her left cheek, Alex would have quickly chilled to the bone, had it not been for Michael riding behind her. She felt sorry for the queen, who, although flanked on either side by stout nobles who would shelter her from the wind, did not have the benefit of a strong man sharing his body heat with her.

As they rounded Hawk Hill and started along the tops towards White Hill and down to Stobs, Alex felt Michael's heart hammer harder in his chest, and his breath come faster.

Despite their fierce argument and the forced betrothal, could it be that Michael still found her attractive?

Some of the tension left her shoulders. Perhaps she could persuade him to join her in Edinburgh after all. *Mayhap there is hope for us yet.*

CHAPTER 30

L UXURIATING IN THE warm water, Alex felt her muscles relax and her worries melt away. Now that Mrs Beattie had stopped fussing and had gone back to attend to the queen, Alex had the room to herself, and she gazed with interest around Michael's chamber.

Simple wooden furniture sat against the walls, but pride of place was given to the four-post bed, hung with heavy drapes and, if she remembered Michael's boast correctly, adorned with a feather mattress. Mrs Beattie had left a drying-cloth and some clean clothes on top of the green coverlet.

The castle was larger—and grander—than she had imagined. Whilst not on the scale of Hermitage, it was solidly built in grey stone, with an impressive vaulted entrance-hall on the ground floor and an oak-panelled great hall above that. A spiral stairway led to the upper chambers, including this one and the one where the queen recovered from her fall.

I hope Her Grace has not caught a chill, Alex thought as she stepped out of the bath and began to dry her damp skin. She herself had recovered quickly, but the queen had suffered the worst during their ordeal and hadn't had the benefit of Michael to warm her on the way to Stobs.

Pulling on yet another set of borrowed clothes, Alex eyed the large bed. It looked so tempting. Could she just give it a try?

Without further consideration, she impetuously flung herself onto the mattress, bouncing softly as she hit the inviting surface. It was delicious. Possibly the most comfortable bed she had ever lain on. *And it could be yours*, a traitorous thought whispered, *if only you weren't so stubborn.*

Michael hesitated outside his chamber. He didn't want to interrupt Alexandra, but he, too, needed clean clothes before they met with the queen again. For their presence had been requested, now that the queen had bathed and dressed.

He rapped on the oak door. "May I come in, Alexandra?"

"Yes," came the reply, and he pushed the door open to find Alexandra sitting on his bed, her hair curling damply around her shoulders and her skin glowing softly in the candle-light.

Even in mis-fitting, borrowed clothes, she was breathtaking.

In two strides he had crossed the room and crushed her into his arms, his lips seeking hers and his hands tangling in her hair. He had acted on instinct, without thought of their estrangement, but to his joy she returned his kiss with passion.

His lips curling with happiness, he pulled her closer for a moment, then took her face in his hands, gazing down at her lustrous eyes and radiant skin.

Under his ardent gaze, she swallowed, nervously wetting her lips. "Sire," she breathed.

"Yes, m'lady?" he touched his lips to hers, then rained butterfly kisses along her jawline until he nuzzled her earlobe. "What would you have me do?"

"Hold me," she whispered.

"I thought you were mad at me?" he teased.

A smile tickled her lips. "Likewise."

His laugh broke some of the tension between them. "Much as I'd like to, we should tarry here no longer. The queen awaits." He pulled her back into his arms for one last kiss, then looked down at her. "Now, Alexandra,"

"Sire, if you're going to kiss me like that," she interrupted, "mayhap we should be less formal. Call me Alex." Her eyelashes fluttered. "My friends do."

He nodded, and touched a finger to the tip of her nose. "*Alex*," he emphasised, then pointed down at their clothing, "we need to dress properly, and go to the queen."

~

Mary sat in a heavy oak chair, her secretary, Maitland, and her lady, Mary Fleming, by her side. Wearing borrowed—but blessedly dry—clothes and wrapped in a blanket, she had finally stopped shivering. A fire glowed in the grate and her hands were wrapped around a posset of wine and milk that warmed her insides. She was ready to face the next part of this long day.

When Michael and Alexandra entered the room, Mary was pleased to notice that he had a possessive hand laid on the small of her back. *Perhaps they have reconciled,* she thought, but kept her face straight.

"I asked you to join me," she looked each of them in the eye, "to extend my gratitude for your 'eroic actions earlier.

You saved my life, and on be'alf of the people of Scotland, I want to 'onour you for your bravery.

"Alexandra," she indicated for the girl to take a step forward. "If it was not for your courage and quick thinking, I would 'ave drowned in that evil mire. As a mark of gratitude, I wish to confer some lands on you—Gilston Peel near Oxton, forfeited by my rebel lords. 'Tis closer to Edinburgh, and will be more convenient for when you work wiz me."

Alexandra gasped. "Your Grace! 'Twas not for reward that I helped you. I would've tried to save anyone—" Her cheeks pinking, she put a hand to her mouth. "Forgive me—I didn't mean to imply that you are just *anyone*, ma'am, but—"

"I understand." Mary stifled a smile at the girl's discomfiture. "But I still wish to compensate you. You could 'ave died. And," this time she allowed herself a smile, "as a landowner, you will become a citizen of Scotland," she glanced sideways at Michael, "which means you are free to marry a Scotsman, should you wish."

Then she turned to her secretary. "Maitland, give me your sword."

Weapon in hand, she stood up. "Cranstoun," she pointed at a point on the floor in front of her. "Please kneel."

The laird's brows creased, but he did as she asked.

"Michael Cranstoun of Stobs, for acts of bravery and loyalty to your sovereign," she tapped him with the flat of the sword, first on the right shoulder, then the left, "I, Mary, Queen of Scots, dub thee knight, in the name of God and in the presence of these witnesses. Arise, Sir Cranstoun."

He blinked at her. "Ma'am?"

Mary flicked upwards with the tip of the sword. "Arise," she repeated.

A dazed look on his face, Michael got to his feet.

"And when—if—you are wed, Alexandra will be Lady

Cranstoun." She raised an eyebrow at the Englishwoman. "Per'aps *that* will convince your father to allow the marriage."

CHAPTER 31

I T WAS WELL past dinner-time when the queen's party finally arrived back in Jedburgh. The queen had borrowed a fresh mount from the stables at Stobs, and Alex was riding Duke once more. She rode wide-eyed through the cobbled marketplace and down towards the queen's house near the river. The town was bigger than she'd imagined; the ruined castle above and the shadows of the hulking abbey below giving the impression of a place of import.

"There are stables behind the orchard." Michael nodded at the stallion. "I will bed him for you, if you wish to join the ladies?"

She shook her head. "It has been a strange day for him," she said, laying a hand on the horse's shoulder. *And strange for me too.* "I'll see to him myself."

Ten minutes later, she had Duke unsaddled and settled in a fresh straw bed, tucking into a manger of oats.

She, for propriety's sake, was to bed in the queen's house, sharing with Libby Preston, since she could not be with Michael until they were wed. *If* they were wed.

What if Father says no? Would she ever see Michael again?

The thought chilled her, and she hurried from Duke's stable —straight into Michael's arms.

Hands circling her waist, he leaned down to kiss her, but she put up a hand to stop him.

"If Father forbids us to marry," she said, the words tumbling out, one on top of another, "will I ever see you again?"

Michael paused, and drew back a little. His face grew serious. "It pains me to say this, but...I dinna know how we could. 'Twould not be right."

Inside her chest, Alex's heart twisted. "But..."

"If we canna be wed, then I daresay your father will find you another. You will be someone else's bride." He traced the outline of her lips with a forefinger. "And I will be a broken man."

She shook her head defiantly, even as his touch sent a delicious shiver down her spine. "I will *not* marry, save to you. But you—you should find another, if we cannot..." A tear trickled down her cheek. "Mayhap that Mary Fleming, who attends the queen. I believe she thinks well of you."

"Aye, Flam. She is a flirt." He tilted Alex's chin towards him and looked her in the eye. "But I dinna care for her. If I canna marry *you*, I wilna marry another. I..." He grimaced. "My heart couldna stand it."

That took Alex's breath away. "But you... We... You hardly know me," she finished in a rush.

In the lamplight, the blue of his eyes was so intense that it burned into her soul. "Mayhap that is true. But I know enough to be sure that my heart is lost to ye, and that I will never love another."

She gasped. "You... You *love* me?"

"Aye. From the first moment I saw ye." His mouth quirked. "Although I thought ye were a laddie, back then. Mayhap from when ye lost that ugly bonnet." He pushed a lock of hair from her forehead and drew her into his arms again. "When I saw your lovely hair and your beautiful face I was lost. Perhaps in time ye can come to love me. I'm a patient man. And I wilna ask," a smile tickled at his lips, "for ye to join me in my big, comfortable, feather bed, until ye feel the same way about me."

At his words, her heart swelled so much that she thought she might burst. "Michael Cranstoun," she started, then corrected herself. "*Sir* Michael Cranstoun, if 'tweren't for my father, I would join you in your big, comfortable, feather bed *right now.*"

He blinked. "So…you… Are ye saying…"

"Yes." She swallowed. "I love you, Michael Cranstoun, even though you are a Scot and the most infuriating man I ever met! I'd marry you tomorrow—if you're happy to live at Gilston, and as long as you'll let me work for the queen."

In answer, Michael swept her into a toe-curling kiss; an embrace that underlined his protestations of love and made her wish that his big feather bed was *here*, rather than miles away at Stobs.

"We'll just have to be sure to persuade your father," he said when they finally broke apart.

"Yes." She would think on it tonight; find the right words to persuade Iron Simon to let her marry a Scotsman. For once she would *prepare*, rather than impetuously saying or doing the first thing that came into her head.

If she was to be Lady Cranstoun, and attend the queen of Scots at court, she would need to learn to control her tongue. *Now is as good a time to start as any.*

CHAPTER 32

THURSDAY 17TH OCTOBER, 1566

ALEX SHOOK HER head groggily and sat up in bed. *What is that infernal noise?* It sounded like someone was trying to break down the front door of the tower house.

Across from her, Libby Preston's face matched the white of her coverlet. "Is it the English?" she asked in a whisper.

I hope not. Alex shook her head. "We'd have heard more noise. An army doesn't come soundlessly into a town this size." Throwing back the blankets, she jumped out of bed. "But whoever it is, we can't be meeting them like this. We should get dressed."

The banging on the door below stopped, and then a few minutes later footsteps pattered up the stone stairs and someone knocked on their door. With no further ado, a servant came in and bowed. "My Lady Graham, the queen requests you join her in the hall."

Alex finished pulling on her boots, then stood up. "Lead on."

Curiosity vying with worry, Alex followed the maid to the great hall on the first floor, then stopped in surprise. "Father!"

In the centre of the room, flanked by Hob and Evan, Iron Simon stood with his legs braced and his knuckles on his hips, facing the queen. Mary, attended by Maitland, Seton, and the ever-present Flam, sat at the head of a large oak table, her auburn hair tied at the back of her head and dark shadows framing her green eyes. At the other end of the table sat Michael with Sir Thomas.

Iron Simon turned at the sound of the door, and the tension left his shoulders. "You are safe!" He gave a satisfied nod. "Now, what is this I'm told about you betrothing yourself to this Scotsman? I'm not having my lands annexed by Scotland." He wiped his hands metaphorically. "Forget him, and marry young Musgrave; a good match that will benefit both our clans."

Alex took a deep breath and waited for her heart to stop racing. *Think before you speak.* This was important, and she needed to use the arguments she'd rehearsed in bed last night, or all would be lost, and the rest of her life—and Michael's—would be ruined.

"Father," she started, looking him in the eye, "you told me once that your marriage to mother was an arranged union; agreed between your father and the Lowthers. They wanted to consolidate the influence of both clans and extend your lands."

Iron Simon gave a curt nod. "That is true. 'Twas a good alliance. As will be yours to Musgrave."

Ignoring that last comment, she clenched her hands together. "And when I was younger, I overheard you one night—in your cups—saying to Evan that you wished you'd been able to marry for love; that Hob's mother would have surely made you happier."

"I never said—"

Alex raised her eyebrows and looked to her uncle. "Is

your memory any better, uncle? Mayhap you had not partaken of so much ale."

Evan grimaced but told the truth. "I recall something of the sort, yes."

With a nod, Alex turned to her father again. "So, from your own words, a marriage for love would be better than one that is merely a marriage of convenience." She straightened her spine. "Michael Cranstoun may be a Scot, but I love him, and he loves me."

Simon's face went hard, and Alex's spirits quailed. "That's as may be," he said with a scowl. "But he is a *Scot*. And you are an English lady; heiress to my keep and lands, destined to lead our clan one day."

"And, married to Michael, I would give you grandsons who could inherit Kersdale and lead the clan. A male heir to keep it in the family." She narrowed her eyes. "Married to Musgrave, there would be no grandsons—no children at all —for he is ugly and gouty, and I would not let him in my bed."

"You would give up your clan—and your birthright—for love?" Simon flicked a dismissive hand at Michael. "What can this man offer you? He is nothing, merely a messenger to the queen."

At this, Michael bristled, and Mary, who had been silent until now, stepped in.

"Lord Graham, Cranstoun is no mere messenger," said the queen. "He is a knight of my realm, and *Sir* Michael is laird of a powerful castle and a clan that prospers, even in these difficult times. 'e would be a good match for any woman."

At this, Simon deflated somewhat.

Alex pressed her advantage. "And yesterday, the queen conferred lands in Scotland on me, for I—we—helped save her life." She put her hands on her hips. "What would you have—a loveless marriage to a fat Englishman producing no grandchildren, or one that would extend our family lands into Scotland and provide heirs to continue your family line?"

CHAPTER 33

LATE OCTOBER, 1566

MICHAEL HAD NOT thought it possible for Alex to look more ravishing than she had at their hand-fasting ceremony. But somehow she had done it.

He had been so proud of her when, with her arguments rather than her temper, she had persuaded her father—however reluctantly—to agree to their union. And now, here they were, in the historic grandeur of Jedburgh Abbey, about to plight their troth.

A vision of loveliness, she floated down the aisle on her father's arm, her face wreathed in smiles and her lovely body adorned by the most beautiful dress of russet and cream satin, encrusted with jewels and embroidered in gold. Tiny cream rosebuds had been set into her hair, which was curled and piled onto the top of her head, emphasising the elegance of her neck and the translucence of her skin.

Sun streamed through the brightly-coloured stained glass windows which dappled their iridescent hues onto the flagstone floor of the nave, so it seemed like Alex walked on a glorious carpet of flowers.

Slipping into place beside him, she took his hand, and it stilled the racing of his heart.

Around them, stone pillars soared and gothic arches leaped, but they could not fly so high or so lightly as his heart. For the woman he loved was beside him, and in a few short moments they would be joined forever.

When it came to the part of the ceremony where they exchanged their vows, Alex looked him in the eye, speaking directly to his soul, as if there was nobody else there. She pledged to love him forever, to care for him always, and even to obey him—although, knowing Alex, she probably had her fingers crossed surreptitiously when she spoke that part.

That thought made him smile, and then it was time for him to give his own vows.

~

The intensity of Michael's gaze when he spoke his vows made Alex's toes curl and her skin tingle. In brand-new doublet and hose, with his freshly washed hair shining like finest gold and his freshly shaven face as smooth as honey, he looked more like a handsome mythical hero then ever before.

But he is my very own hero. The man who had saved her life, helped save her from Bothwell, and captured her heart forever. And she was so proud of him—he was laird of a castle, deputy warden of the Borders, and protector of the queen. Life with him would never be boring, she was sure, and she couldn't wait for that life together to start.

As the priest intoned the final words and pronounced that they were now married in the sight of God and the church, Michael swept her into an embrace that for decorum's sake was brief, but still managed to weaken her knees and take her breath away.

She had almost regained her composure by the time they turned to face the congregation, ready to proceed out of the church as man and wife.

Then Michael leaned towards her and whispered huskily in her ear, "Did I tell ye, lass—I canna *wait* to get ye into that big, comfortable, feather bed!"

Her heart fluttered, even as she flashed him an impish grin and squeezed his hand. "Likewise."

EPILOGUE

A T THE KNOCK on his chamber door, Bothwell raised his head from the pillow, keeping his eyelids closed for a moment till the pain in his head receded and he could bear the light of day. "What?" he growled, opening his eyes to see his wife Jean, who had entered the room almost silently and hovered at his bedside.

"The doctor is downstairs," she said, twitching the skirts of her brown day dress, and not meeting his eyes. "He wants to bleed you again."

"Bleed me? The man is a leech! I will have no blood left if he bleeds me again."

She wrinkled her nose. "My lord, I'm sure the physician knows best."

"And *I'm* sure he's just trying to line his purse at my expense!" The earl banged a fist on the firmly-stuffed mattress. "Send him away!"

"My lord—" Jean protested, but Bothwell cut her off.

"Now!" he roared.

With a sniff, Jean turned and flounced out of the room, pulling the heavy door shut behind her with a thud.

Bothwell grimaced, but not from the headache this time. *She is like a brown chicken, scratching in the dirt and peck-peck-pecking. Constantly pecking at me.* As the sister of the Earl of Huntly, she'd seemed like a good match when he'd married her, but now he was not so sure.

After spending so much time at court, it was hard not to compare Jean to the ladies he'd met there—especially the queen. And compared to dull, homespun Jean, Mary was like a magnificent, newly-woven tapestry, with her glowing auburn hair, perfect white skin and bright-enamelled jewels.

A woman like that would look well on my arm, or sat beside me in my great hall.

Casting his eyes around the grey stone walls of his room, Bothwell's gaze returned to the turned-oak posts of his bed and the woollen blankets that covered his body. *Or waiting for me under the covers.* His thin lips curved upwards at the image painted by his imagination.

Yes.

I am with the wrong woman. I deserve better than this. He nodded, mind made up.

Smoothing the linen sheet that lay over his chest, he touched his thumb to one finger at a time as he made his plans.

First I need my wounds to heal. It would take time, but he was strong. He *would* get better soon. Doctor or no doctor.

Next he should get himself back into favour at court, usurping the bastard Moray and the grey weasel Maitland to get the ear of the queen.

After that, divorcing Jean should be easy.

And then all that remained was the king... who might conveniently drink or whore himself to death sometime soon, if Bothwell was lucky. But if not, perhaps with a carefully placed prompt, or a reminder of Darnley's collusion in the plot to kill Riccio, the queen could be persuaded to get rid of the embarrassing sot…

He almost laughed at the thought.

When I am better, I will have her, he vowed. *One way or another, one step at a time.* She would be his, and he would be…

King!

~

THE END

~

Want to read more about Mary Queen of Scots and the lords and ladies of her court?

Get the next book, **A Love Beyond**:

~

Read on for a sample:

AN EXCERPT FROM A LOVE BEYOND

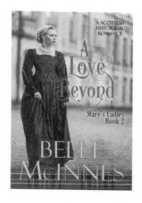

TUESDAY 15TH OCTOBER, 1566

Standing to the right of the queen at the far end of the banqueting hall, Libby was in prime position to observe the French ambassador and his attendants as they opened the heavy oak door and stepped into the room.

Heels tapping across the polished floor, the ambassador crossed the room, removed his hat, and bowed low before the queen, velvet robes flowing around his knees. A stout man with a guarded face, pointed beard and hair that was more reminiscent of salt than pepper, he greeted the queen in French. "Enchantée, majesté."

Behind him came a middle-aged, plain-faced man wearing eyeglasses, and then a young man who was so handsome, the sight of him stopped the breath in Libby's throat, and sucked all the air from the room. For a moment, she thought she might swoon.

Tall, olive-skinned and dark-haired, he wore a dashing outfit of rich brown, gold and cream, which emphasised his lean frame and powerful muscles. But it was his smile as he bowed before the queen that bewitched Libby. Wide and unaffected, his full lips twitched up at the corners, making his brown eyes sparkle with warmth and a hint of mischief. *Here is a lord whose heart I might wish to win.*

With a flourish, the ambassador introduced his companions to the queen. "Your Grace, may I present to you my secretary, Monsieur Édouard McMann, and my physician, Monsieur Robert Nau."

Or not a lord. Libby's shoulders drooped. Here stood the first man who had quickened her pulse since she arrived at court, and he had no title. Was this the way it was to be? That the only eligible lord to take an interest in her would bore her to tears, and anyone who made her heart sing would be unavailable to her?

In comparison to Monsieur Nau, whose expression almost glowed with curiosity and intelligence, Hugh Somerville's moon face seemed pasty, lifeless and bland. *But he will be the seventh lord of Somerville one day, and laird of Couthally castle. I must keep my purpose in mind.* With a heavy sigh, she turned her attention back to the queen.

~

Rising from his bow, Robert gazed with admiration at the queen. She was beautiful, like he'd been told. Tall —taller than usual for a woman, and taller than many men— she carried herself with graciousness and elegance. *As I'd expect from one brought up in France.* Auburn hair framed an oval face with perfect white skin, fine lips and expressive green eyes.

And those eyes crinkled at the corners as the queen greeted them. "Bonsoir, gentlemen," she said, and swept an arm around the room. "The court of Scotland welcomes you. Please make yourselves known to my lords and ladies. Refreshments will be served momentarily."

Murmurs of conversation began to fill the air as, from a doorway in the far corner of the room, liveried servants appeared bearing trays of wine and sweetmeats.

Robert took this opportunity to scrutinise the soberly dressed men and more colourful ladies arrayed around the banqueting hall. Most of the men were older, and some eyed the ambassador from under lowered brows. *Mayhap these are the Protestant lords McMann told me about.* Nearer the queen stood her ladies, some of whom rivalled the monarch herself in looks and finery. But it was the younger fair-haired maid to the left of the queen who caught his eye. With hair the colour of spun gold, a heart-shaped face and lips that could grace a cherub, she wore a stunning— and daring—blue gown that emphasised the azure of her eyes.

"Welcome to Scotland, Monsieur Nau," said a husky voice at his elbow, tearing his attention away from the beautiful maid. "I am Mary Fleming—or Flam, as most call me." Her eyes flashed at him in an unspoken signal that he read as easily as he read his medical textbooks. *She flirts with me.* On another day he might have found himself taken with her full figure and dark looks. But compared to the intriguing blonde she seemed brazen and obvious.

He kissed her hand. "A pleasure to meet you, mademoiselle."

Flam fluttered her eyelashes at him, then indicated a white-haired, black-eyed man behind her, with a face whose red nose and thready veins bespoke of a penchant for alcohol. "Monsieur Jacques Lusgerie, the queen's physician, wanted to meet you. I am sure you will have much to talk about."

"Delighted to make your acquaintance." Robert clasped the older man's hand, but his grip was limp, like a half-dead fish.

"You studied in Paris?" Lusgerie asked, without preamble.

"Oui. Under André Vésale, God rest his soul. You knew him?"

"Only by reputation." Lusgerie's lips narrowed. "I don't have time for new-fangled ideas like his." He crossed his arms on top of his ample paunch. "For over twenty years I've been physician to the queen—since her childhood in France —and I've had little need of anything save bloodletting and purging."

Robert kept his expression neutral. "Her Grace must value your experience."

Flam intervened. "We should not monopolise you, Monsieur Lusgerie." She caught Robert's eye and lifted her chin in the direction of the other ladies. "Let me introduce you to my friends."

A moment later, Robert found himself inclining his head before the fair-haired beauty, who Flam introduced as Lady Libby Logan of Preston.

"Enchantée, Mademoiselle Logan," he said, taking her hand, pleased to notice a catch in her breath at his touch. Holding her gaze, he bent his lips to her fingers, marvelling at how this slightest of contacts made his skin tingle and his pulse race. *Does she feel it too?* As he straightened and reluctantly dropped her hand, colour rose in her cheeks, giving him his answer. *Oui.*

Before Flam presented him to the next lady, Robert found his mind wandering, dreaming about what it might be like to get to know Libby better, to hold her, caress her, kiss her... and to give her pleasure in the ways he had learned while growing up in Paris.

For he had understood from an early age that women deserved to be cherished, adored and satisfied; and he had been taught by the ladies at his mother's establishment that the man who would unselfishly seek their enjoyment before his own would ultimately gain a far bigger bounty than his imagination could ever conjure. What would it be like, to win the heart of a maid such as Libby?

And then reason reasserted itself.

This comely Scottish mademoiselle, however beautiful and tempting she might be, was a noble lady, and out of reach to one such as him. He needed to remember his place, and his purpose here. He needed to build his reputation and his fortune, so that he could help the deserving people of his hometown. And so he needed to forget any foolish notion of loving a Scots noblewoman, for it would get him nowhere, and drive him to madness in the process.

∼

Want to find out what happens next?
Get the next book, **A Love Beyond**:

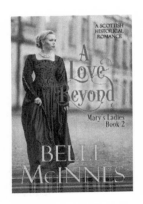

A NOTE ON THE HISTORY

WRITING A HISTORICAL novel is always a challenge. For every history book you read, there are a dozen more that you *could* read. And every third book you read will contradict things that were said in the two that preceded it... So which do you believe? And when do you stop?

The thing about history is that if you weren't actually *there*, you can't know *exactly* what happened—or why—unless someone has written it down, or some archaeologist has dug up evidence. And even then, can we be sure it's true? We all know the saying that history is written by the victors, and everyone has his (or her) point of view, usually biased...

THE HISTORICAL CHARACTERS IN MY BOOK

To avoid conflicting with *real* history, the main characters (Alex and Michael) are fictional, as are most of the side characters like Hob Forster or Iron Simon. However, the remainder of the cast are actual people from history—the Queen, Bothwell, Mary Fleming, the wardens.

The events in this book that relate to the Queen and

Bothwell are real too—she really *did* rush from Jedburgh via Stobs Castle to Hermitage to visit him after he'd been injured in a fight with Little Jock Elliot; she fell in a bog, and nearly died. I've just added scenes from Alex and Michael's lives around those very *real* historical events.

WARRING FAMILIES

Border history made some of my decisions more challenging, though. For example, not much is known of the Deputy Wardens, which gave me fairly free rein to choose who Michael would be. I wanted him to be from one of the major families of the Scottish Middle March—but not a Kerr, as his warden was a Kerr and that would be confusing.

So I initially had him as a Scott (an early member of the famous Sir Walter Scott's family). Then I researched castles that belonged to the Scotts where the ownership in 1566 was unclear (so that it could've been his), and had intended him to be laird of Aikwood Tower near Selkirk, which was refurbished in recent times by the famous Scottish Member of Parliament, Lord David Steel.

...until I read a little more, and discovered that the Scotts and Kerrs had been mortal enemies until 1572 when they'd finally been united by marriage. So there was no way Walter Kerr would've chosen a Scott as his deputy! Back to the drawing board!

This time I started with the castles, looking for a suitable seat for Michael which would work with the geography of the story. Stobs Castle on the direct route between Hermitage and Jedburgh was the ideal candidate, for it was owned by the Cranstoun family until around 1607 when it passed to the Elliots. But it was destroyed by fire in 1712 and all the family papers were burned, so little is known of its early history—ideal from my point of view!

FURTHER READING

For readers who are interested to know more of the historical setting of this book, there are a couple of very readable non-fiction books which will let you learn more about the reivers and the wardens:

- *The Steel Bonnets* by George MacDonald Fraser
- *The Reivers* by Alistair Moffat

To learn more about Mary Queen of Scots, the best books I've found are:

- *Mary Queen of Scots and the Murder of Lord Darnley* by Alison Weir
- *Mary Queen of Scots* by Antonia Fraser

Novels set in this period of Scottish history are not too common, and are not always historically accurate, but here are a few I've found:

- *A Famine of Horses* (Sir Robert Carey Mystery Series) by P F Chisholm
- *Reiver* by David Pilling
- *The Marchman* by Nigel Tranter
- *Warden of the Queen's March* by Nigel Tranter
- *Fair Border Bride* by Jen Black

GLOSSARY

Assizes: A travelling justice court (see Eyres)

Baldrick: A diagonal belt, worn from shoulder to hip, to support a sword

Bastle House: A fortified house, often a farmhouse

Borders (The Borders): The southern counties of Scotland, adjacent to the border with England

Burn (eg Braidley Burn): A stream

Close: A narrow alleyway between houses (see Pend)

Cramoisie: Crimson/purple

Day of Truce: The monthly meeting of the Wardens of the Scottish and English Marches, where they would dispense justice

Dirk: Dagger

Doglock rifle: An early firearm

Drove Road: A track used by shepherds and cattle herders to take stock to market

Drystane dyke: A wall made of rough stones placed together without mortar

Eyres: A circuit made by an itinerant judge (see Assizes)

Garron: A small, sturdy Scottish pony (see Hobbler)

Gavotte: An old French dance

Glen: A Scottish valley

Half armour: Steel breastplate

Hand-fasting: A formal promise of marriage, signified by the joining of hands and making of promises

Hobbler: A small, sturdy Borders pony (see Garron)

Hot Trod: The legal pursuit of reivers with the aim of catching them red-handed. Signified by the carrying of a burning turf on the point of a spear, and valid for up to six days after the robbery, after which it was called a 'cold trod'

Keep: Castle or tower (see Peel)

Kinsmen: Family or clansmen

Knowe (eg Swire Knowe): Hill

Lords of the Congregation: A group of Protestant lords who plotted against the queen

Marches: The areas Scotland and England adjacent to the Border. Each country had East, Middle and West Marches

Mizzle: Misty drizzle.

Osprey: A large bird of prey.

Palfrey: A riding horse particularly suitable for a woman.

Peel House, Peel Tower: A fortified, stone-built tower (see Keep)

Pend: An alleyway between houses (see Close)

Portcullis: Iron grating designed to slide down and prevent entrance to a castle.

Posset: A warm drink of wine and curdled milk

Privy Council: A body of advisers appointed by the sovereign

Reiver: A thieving rider.

Shieling: A rough shelter on or near a grazing ground

Turnpike (stair): A spiral staircase

Warden (of the Marches): Official in charge of dispensing justice in the Borderlands (see Day of Truce)

CHARACTERS

Names in **bold** are real historical characters.

Alexander, Lord Home: warden of the Scottish East March
Alexandra Graham: Daughter of Simon and heiress to Kersdale Keep
Archie (o' the Bell) **Armstrong of Whithaugh**: Reiver
Mrs (Beth) Beattie: Michael's housekeeper
Dod **Armstrong of Mangerton**: notorious reiver
Duke: Alex's horse
Evan Graham: Simon's brother, Alex's uncle.
Francis Russell, Earl of Bedford: Warden of the English East March
George Gordon, 5ᵗʰ Earl of Huntly
George Seton, 7ᵗʰ Lord Seton: half-brother of Mary Seton and Master of the Queen's household
Henry, Lord Scrope: Warden of the English West March
Henry Stewart, Lord Darnley: Mary's husband and cousin
Hob Forster: Alex's friend
James Hepburn, Earl of Bothwell: Member of Mary's Privy Council

James Stewart, Earl of Moray: Mary's half-brother, illegitimate son of James V, member of her Privy Council

Lady Jean Gordon: Bothwell's wife and Huntly's sister

Jupiter: Mary Queen of Scots' dog

Little Jock Elliot of the Park: Notorious reiver

Sir John Forster: Warden of the English Middle March

Sir John Maxwell: Warden of the Scottish West March

Libby (Elizabeth) Logan of Preston: Lady-in-Waiting to Mary Queen of Scots

Mary Beaton (Beth): Lady-in-Waiting to Mary Queen of Scots

Mary Fleming (Flam): Lady-in-Waiting to Mary Queen of Scots

Mary Livingston (Livvy): Lady-in-Waiting to Mary Queen of Scots

Mary Seton (Ebba): Lady-in-Waiting to Mary Queen of Scots

Mary Stuart, Queen of Scots

Michael Cranstoun: Deputy Warden of the Scottish Middle March, laird of Penchrise and Master of Stobs Castle

Mist: Michael's favourite horse

Peter Forster: Bondman to Simon Graham

Robert Elliot of the Shaws: leader of the Elliots

Iron Simon Graham: Alex's father, Lord of Kersdale

Spirit: Michael's horse

Sir Thomas Kerr, Laird of Ferniehirst

Tom Turnbull: Michael's liegeman

Sir Walter Ker: Warden of the Scottish Middle March

William Livingstone, 6th Lord Livingston: Brother of Mary Fleming and member of the Privy Council

William Maitland of Lethington: Mary's Secretary

ABOUT THE AUTHOR

A native Scot who lives in the hinter-
land between Edinburgh and the
Borders, Belle loves to write about
Scotland and its history.

In addition to writing historical
romance, she rides dressage, teaches
skiing—and pens prize-winning urban fantasy, sci-fi and
contemporary romance as Roz Marshall, and page-turning
cozy mysteries as R.B. Marshall.

Find out more about Belle and her upcoming books by
joining her newsletter: subscribepage.com/joinbelle

ALSO BY

BY BELLE MCINNES:

Mary's Ladies

Scottish Historical Romance telling the story of Mary Queen of Scots:

- *A Love Divided*
- *A Love Beyond*
- *A Love Concealed (releasing 31 Aug 2020)*

BY BELLE MCINNES, WRITING AS R.B MARSHALL:

The **Highland Horse Whisperer** series

Cozy Mystery set in Scotland (and London for the prequel):

- The Secret Santa Mystery
- A Corpse at the Castle
- A Right Royal Revenge (releasing 30 Sept 2020)
- A Henchman at the Highland Games (due in 2020)

BY BELLE MCINNES, WRITING AS ROZ MARSHALL:

The **Celtic Fey** series

Urban Fantasy / Young Adult Fantasy set in Scotland (and the faerie realm):

- Unicorn Magic
- Kelpie Curse

- Faerie Quest
- The Celtic Fey (Books 1-3, paperback or eBook)
- The Fey Bard

Secrets in the Snow *series*

Sports Romance / Women's Fiction set in a Scottish ski school:

- Winter Arrives
- Skiing with Santa
- A Dream for Hogmanay
- Fear of Falling
- The Snow Patrol
- My Snowy Valentine
- The Racer Trials
- Snow Blind
- Weathering the Storm
- Secrets in the Snow - the Complete Season (paperback or eBook)

Half Way Home *stories*

Young Adult Science Fiction set in Hugh Howey's *Half Way Home* universe:

- Nobody's Hero
- The Final Solution

Scottish stories:

- Still Waters

BIBLIOGRAPHY

NON-FICTION:

Ball, Krista D. *What Kings Ate and Wizards Drank*

Bingham, Madeleine. *Scotland Under Mary Stuart - an Account of Everyday Life*

Colburn, H, (1842) *Letters of Mary, Queen of Scots: And Documents Connected with Her Personal History*

Coventry, Martin. *The Castles of Scotland*

Fraser, Antonia. *Mary Queen of Scots*

Fraser, George MacDonald. *The Steel Bonnets*

Hale, John. *Mary Queen of Scots*

Hermitage Castle, Official Guide (Historic Scotland)

In Search of the Border Reivers (map by Ordnance Survey)

Jedburgh Abbey, Official Guide (Historic Scotland)

Marshall, Rosalind K. *Queen Mary's Women*

Mayhew, Mickey. *The Little Book of Mary Queen of Scots*

Moffat, Alistair. *The Reivers*

Musgrave, Thea. *Mary, Queen of Scots: An Opera in Three Acts*

Oddy, Zilla. *Mary Queen of Scots' House, Jedburgh: A Look at the Building and Its Inhabitants*

Pease, Howard. *The Lord Wardens of the Marches of England and Scotland*

Pocket Scottish History: story of a nation (Lomond)

Ross, David. *Scotland: History of a Nation*

Schiern, Frederik. *Life of James Hepburn, Earl of Bothwell*

Small, John. *Queen Mary at Jedburgh in 1566*

Thomson, Thomas (1768-1852). *Diurnal of Occurrents - from a manuscript of the sixteenth century*

Stedall, Robert. *The Challenge to the Crown, Vol 1*

Weir, Alison: *Mary Queen of Scots and the Murder of Lord Darnley*

Many web articles and wikipedia entries

FICTION:

Black, Jen. *Fair Border Bride*

Pilling, David. *Reiver*

Tranter, Nigel. *The Marchman*

Tranter, Nigel. *Warden of the Queen's March*

ACKNOWLEDGMENTS

I am indebted to Andrea, Wendy and Larry, my proofreading and beta-reading team, who added extra polish and value to my scribblings.

Thanks also to Bob, who has supported me through this experiment into a new genre, and whose love for history was a part of the inspiration for the series.